THE SUMMERHOUSE GHOST

Lizzie is thrilled when her theatre company gets the chance to put on an open-air production at a Georgian country house. As soon as she sees the property she's enchanted by it — and by two of the residents: Griffin, and his foster son, Oscar.

But the house has secrets, and something within it starts to threaten the play, Lizzie's new relationships, and her safety. Something in the house wishes her harm . . .

CAMILLA KELLY

THE SUMMERHOUSE GHOST

Complete and Unabridged

LINFORD
Leicester

First published in Great Britain in 2020

First Linford Edition
published 2021

A catalogue record for this book is available
from the British Library.

ISBN 978–1–4448–4734–5

Published by
Ulverscroft Limited
Anstey, Leicestershire

Printed and bound in Great Britain by
TJ Books Ltd., Padstow, Cornwall

This book is printed on acid-free paper

1

April. Lizzie was lost. Lost and trespassing. But only a little bit.

She knew Waverley wouldn't really mind if he caught her on his land. Being lost, though, that part surprised her. The estate wasn't particularly big. No matter where you were in the gardens or wood, you could usually see the great chimney stacks of the Georgian house, or a glimpse of white façade.

And yet.

She'd lost her bearings. She thought she'd followed the same path through the gardens that she'd taken the last time she was here, but she'd never seen this little copse of pine trees before. Each crunching footstep she made in the pristine early-morning snow was both a delight (she loved that sound!) and a clarion of her guilt.

Sensing that easy-going Waverley wouldn't mind her being here wasn't quite the same as having permission, after all.

Maybe he'd wanted to be the one to break the fresh snow. He seemed to Lizzie the type to make snow angels, despite being a seventy-six-year-old in a trilby. And the lord of the manor surely had the right to reserve those kinds of pleasures for himself, didn't he? Along with first dibs on the winning Victoria sponge at the village fair and being the one to put the star at the top of the Christmas tree.

She paused to readjust her woolly hat over her ears, tucking back a curl of hair. Her photocopied map made no sense at all. She stared at it in bewilderment, her breath misting in front of her face and her fingertips tingling despite her gloves. The air here was lovely, as sweet as crystallised ginger. And the quiet! Nothing but pigeons cooing and the distant hum of traffic. It thrilled Lizzie to her bones.

Passing through the copse, she came to another snow-laden lawn, edged by a gravel path and a row of silver limes. The trees were tall and slender, their long rhythmical shadows on the white lawn like the black keys of a piano.

This was the spot!

This was the spot where their small theatre company would be putting on an open-air production of *Alice's Adventures in Wonderland* in the summer.

Lizzie couldn't believe her luck.

She felt such an affinity with the place. There was a timeless air about it that excited her dreamy imagination — she could almost see the gentlemen in their morning coats and the ladies in their bustles sashaying along the avenue or stealing into the folly for a romantic rendezvous.

The lawn was perfect for people to spread their picnic blankets and watch the play. The summerhouse would store all their equipment and serve as a backdrop for the stage. Lizzie, as stage manager and set designer as well as the writer, had already spent months planning every detail. She was desperate not to let anyone down — especially her sister Meredith, who had been dreaming of an opportunity to direct a play for years.

The whole scene made her heart beat faster.

In her pocket she found her silver sixpence, and she ran her fingers over the worn edges. A little seed of doubt crept in.

Was this too good to be true?

Everything was falling into place: first the grant from the arts council — not a lot, but enough; then other professionals, connections of Meredith's, being available and willing to join the company. And then Edmund Waverley offering the location, which turned out to be the perfect backdrop for the stage.

This was really going to happen. Lizzie's play was going to be performed here in a few months.

'Oh.'

She sat down with a bump in the snow.

People would sit around on pull-out chairs and picnic blankets. They'd share a bottle of wine, buy ice cream for the kids. They'd glance warily at the temperamental sky.

They'd listen to every word she wrote. Her name would be in the programme and everything: *Writer and Producer — Lizzie Palmerstone.*

She hunched forward, her elbows on her knees, covering her cold ears with her hands.

What was I thinking? What if it's terrible? What if no one comes?

She took some deep breaths and tried to let her natural optimism reassert itself. Meredith was always telling her off for letting her imagination run away with her. It could be a negative as well as a positive.

Glancing up, she almost blamed her overactive imagination for conjuring up a little elf when she saw a small boy crossing the path at the edge of the lawn and disappearing behind some rhododendrons. But the child was carrying a very un-elf-like sports rucksack that was almost as big as he was; his thumbs were tucked under the straps and his body bent forward to counterbalance the weight.

5

Intrigued, Lizzie followed. He was headed towards the folly. A short flight of steps led down to its foundations, a dark recess below ground level.

At the bottom of the steps, amid an unruly, neglected patch of undergrowth, the child was covering over a shallow hole with earth. Finishing, he scattered a few leaves over the spot to disguise the disturbance. His mop of dull brown hair fell about his face, and he pushed it out of his eyes impatiently. It was desperate for a cut.

As he flicked his head back he caught sight of her. For a second he looked frightened. Amber eyes widened in a pale, freckled face. Lizzie judged he was about seven or eight.

'Hi.' She smiled.

He relaxed a bit. No smile, though. He looked at her with big, solemn eyes, as if trying to decide whether her stumbling upon him doing something sneaky was something he needed to worry about.

Before she could tell him his secret was safe with her, they heard a man shout from the path above.

'Oscar!'

Lizzie almost laughed at the boy's uh-oh expression. She met his gaze and slowly raised a finger to her lips.

A pause while he considered her with those solemn eyes that seemed an age older than his freckles. Another flick of his head to get that long hair back. Then he raised a finger to his lips too . . . and smiled. Such an unexpectedly sweet smile that Lizzie was floored.

What a sweetheart.

He lifted his massive bag onto his shoulder and took off towards the voice. Lizzie waited a few moments before following.

She saw the boy walking beside a man on the avenue ahead of her, heading to the house. A removal van was parked in the driveway, men in overalls carrying boxes and furniture into a side entrance, which Lizzie knew led to the part of the house that had been converted into flats.

She watched the two figures as she trailed behind them. Neither spoke.

There was a tension in the way the man held himself, as though he was bracing himself for something. She saw his profile as he turned to the boy. His dark hair parted in shining waves against the breeze.

He dropped a hand onto the boy's slender shoulder, hesitantly but with tenderness. It was just a fleeting touch. As if they didn't quite know how to be with one another. But that touch . . . Lizzie knew love when she saw it.

When they reached the house, the boy went inside with his bag and the man was left alone. He was rigid as steel, feet planted on the gravel driveway, gazing out towards the sea.

All day she thought about the garden and the place she'd found for her play. And she thought too of the handsome stranger, and how he'd taken a long, slow breath before entering the house.

2

August. Griff Lennox knew it was going to be a long day when he tried to leave the house and ended up in the library.

He sighed, and tried again to make it to his car, concentrating this time. The problem was, he had too much on his mind to be on his guard against the tricksy house. And now, as well as being burdened, he was exasperated too. Not a good way to start the day.

But he was the one who had chosen to come back here after all, knowing it was the best place to bring up a child. It was worth it if it meant he could see a smile on Oscar's serious little face occasionally.

Although, now that it was the start of the school holidays, he had another set of problems to worry about.

Oscar had been living with him for four months and their lives still didn't seem to be running smoothly. He had to keep reminding himself to give it time.

He went in search of Waverley to confirm their arrangements for the day. Thankfully Waverley, as well as being a tolerant landlord, was an enthusiastic babysitter.

Griff found him standing outside the west wing of the building, staring at a pear tree heavy with blossom, as if completely spellbound by the mystery of nature. Griff stopped beside him.

'Morning, old man,' Waverley said, still staring at the tree. After a moment he rubbed his chin. As usual he was dressed in an open-necked shirt and a tweedy jacket, looking a bit like a retired geography teacher; as usual his battered old lace-up shoes gave him away for the working country gent he was.

'Morning. Just checking you're still ok to keep an eye on Oscar today?'

'Of course.'

'Thanks, Waverley. I appreciate it.'

There was a shout as Oscar came rushing out of the house, still pulling on a T-shirt. He raced up to them, doing a funny little skidding stop like a boy in a cartoon. Griff wondered if Oscar knew how entertaining he was sometimes. He suspected not.

'Are you leaving?' Oscar asked. Was it in case Griff had changed his mind about going to work, Griff wondered? A bit of wishful thinking?

'I've got to make a quick trip into town, then I'll be back here at the restaurant, and I'll be finished by six.'

'Promise?'

Though he'd had a haircut recently, Oscar still had a nervous habit of flicking his hair back. It hardly ever made a difference, the mop settling flat to his scalp again straight away. Now though, in the sun, Griff could see red gold glitters among the dull brown, like pennies in a wishing well.

'I'll do my best, O,' Griff said gently.

Oscar didn't seem fully reassured. His upturned freckled face was wistful, a glimmer of something in his eyes that filled Griff with both pride and pity. Budding hero worship. Poor kid. What grim twist of fate had made Griff such a strong influence on him?

'Why don't you go and see Claudette?' Griff suggested to Oscar. 'She's baking cakes this morning. I'm sure she could do with a taster.'

Oscar nodded and trailed off towards the convertedbarn where the restaurant was housed, not even smiling at the thought of the chef's fresh cakes. There it was, thought Griff with discomfort, touching a hand to his chest: that little tug on his heart that was becoming more and more familiar. Exactly the sort of thing he'd been resisting.

'A difficult child to make happy,' Waverley remarked.

Don't I know it.

'Some special occasion for the cakes?' Waverley asked.

'Didn't you say the theatre company arrives today?' When Waverley raised an eyebrow in surprise, Griff added, 'What? You asked me to be nice.'

'And I appreciate it. I know you've got a lot going on.' He patted Griff's shoulder. 'They're working on the east lawn and rehearsing in the summer-house,' Waverley said. 'They shouldn't be a bother to you.'

Griff just grunted. He understood why Waverley had given his permission for them to use the grounds, he even grudgingly admired Waverley's plans to hire out Hartley for such things. A house this size needed to earn its keep. Although it had belonged to Waverley's ancestors for generations, it had only come back into his family's possession twenty years ago, when Waverley bought it back — in a slightly dilapidated state — from an impoverished historical trust. Waverley had done it up, converted the fire-damaged west wing into apartments for rent, and thought about ways to make an income without compromising the house's integrity. One of those ways had been to offer Griff the chance to run his own restaurant on the property.

Griff admired the way Waverley was trying to make the house into a business. He just wanted things kept simple.

'Griffin?' Waverley said as Griff started to leave, in that way of his, every letter perfectly shaped.

Griff turned back. Waverley was still staring at the tree. 'Do you know anything about this?' Waverley said. 'Nope.' 'Hmm.'

He was saved by his mobile phone ringing, but the relief was short-lived when he saw the name on the screen. His accountant.

'Bye, then,' he called to Waverley, letting the phone ring a couple more times while he headed out of hearing. He felt Waverley watch him go.

Of course he knew about the tree. He'd even seen it appear one evening last week.

Who would have suspected that the tree wasn't a tree? That, in fact, it was just one more of Griff's ghosts, lingering around this house.

★   ★   ★

The two months that Lizzie was away from Hartley she dreamed of it constantly. Some were anxiety dreams, granted, when she was rigged up in stocks on the spot where the stage should be and pelted with rotten fruit. But some were peaceful and reassuring, as if she belonged to the house somehow and it welcomed her in.

And some . . . some had the black-haired stranger.

He was always in the distance. No matter how she tried, she couldn't get any closer to him. Still, she'd feel reassured by his presence, just by the fact he was there, with her. Each time she woke from one of these dreams it was with a pining feeling, like homesickness.

She'd made a couple of trips to the house over the last week or two to discuss details with Waverley and show him the location she'd chosen — which he thankfully approved. But she never saw him.

Today was the first day all the cast and crew would see Hartley. They'd have two weeks to rehearse and build the set — nothing fancy — before a week of performances.

Lizzie arrived early that morning, wanting to be there to greet everyone else as they arrived. It was a warm sunny day. She parked at the front of the house and tumbled out of her little car, its back seat piled high with folders and notes, clasping a flask of coffee. Lizzie had actors, a director, and a set builder, but almost every other task fell to her. Meredith was doubling as director and Queen of Hearts. That meant, Lizzie thought with a wry smile, double the drama.

She was thinking about her sister — and, yes, the handsome stranger sometimes too, wondering if she'd see him again — when a yellow sports car came joyously whizzing up the driveway, spun to a stop, and Meredith herself emerged from it.

Meredith could still amaze her.

Climbing from the passenger seat, Meredith put one stiletto heel on the ground, then the other, then leaned back into the car to blow the driver a kiss before sauntering over to Lizzie with a wicked smile.

'You're a bit overdressed,' Lizzie noted.

Meredith glanced down at her jewelled skinny jeans and silver top. She might be wearing last night's clothes but she looked as gorgeous as always. Even her hair, several shades blonder than Lizzie's, was perfectly styled. And Lizzie doubted it had even been brushed that morning.

Lizzie couldn't envy her sister for being beautiful. Meredith wasn't beautiful. They both knew that. Her forehead was large and her nose was long. But what Meredith had was more potent than beauty: an indefinable charisma that drew men to her. As if she was an ancient world goddess with favours to bestow. And her most powerful asset of all: a voice that could be like anything, from your first forbidden taste of alcohol, to a choirboy's purest note — and it turned men to jelly.

And not only men. When she was on

stage you couldn't take your eyes off her.

At thirty-one, Meredith was three years older than Lizzie, but she didn't look it.

Meredith helped herself to Lizzie's coffee and drawled in that million-dollar voice, 'There's no such thing as over-dressed.'

A young gardener, who'd been carrying a ladder past the entrance of the house, was so busy staring, he tripped over the bottom rung.

Lizzie turned so he couldn't see her laugh.

'Please be careful. Our insurance only covers our own staff.'

Meredith was delighted. She gave the boy a wave and the poor thing turned so scarlet Lizzie thought he might explode.

That was what Lizzie envied her for. The ability to wrap any man around her little finger. What must that be like, Lizzie wondered?

She'd grown used to living in Meredith's shadow and most of the time was content to be anonymous, but occasionally, just occasionally, on particular people, she'd love just a taste of that power.

'Why didn't you introduce me to your driver?' Lizzie said as the car pulled away.

'I don't know his name.'

Lizzie put on her scandalised face.

'He only gave me a lift,' Meredith said. 'He's a friend of a friend, that's all. Really, Liz, I'm not half as bad as you think I am.'

'You don't know how bad I think you are.'

'You've turned into grandma while I've been gone!' She peered more closely at Lizzie. 'And what's going on with your eyebrows?'

Typical sister. 'Thanks for pointing that out. Plucking mishap. I don't want to talk about it.'

'Honestly, I can't leave you alone for five minutes, can I?'

Grinning, Meredith pulled Lizzie into a hug. 'Did you miss me?'

For the last two months she'd been away as part of a touring theatre company. Lizzie had felt every minute of her absence. She extended the hug, holding her sister tight. 'Not a bit.'

Laughing, Meredith turned to take a long look at the house.

'Great place. Does it have ghosts?'

'Wouldn't that be fantastic?' Lizzie sighed.

'No! Are you crazy?'

'Don't worry. I'm sure they'd be friendly.'

'How many people live here?'

'I'm not sure. The west wing has been converted into apartments, and the old barn is a restaurant now.'

'Is that one of the tenants?' Meredith nodded past Lizzie's shoulder to a man rounding the house and heading towards his car. 'Or one of the lords?'

Lizzie turned.

It was him.

He talked into his mobile phone as he walked, his long strides making the distance short.

'Yeah. I saw, I think, yeah. Yes. A tenant,' Lizzie said.

He noticed them, and lifted his hand

to wave in greeting. Lizzie and Meredith both waved back in unison.

'Seems nice,' Meredith said.

* * *

Mid-morning, with the welcome speeches over with, and everyone seemingly delighted with the setting for the stage, Lizzie looked up and saw the little boy she'd met back in April trotting towards her across the grass after a thin, quick-stepping woman, both of them carrying trays.

One by one, everyone around Lizzie dropped what they were doing. Even the actors who had been in the summerhouse with Meredith, picking through trunks of costumes, suddenly found themselves drawn back to the west lawn. They all stared.

'Good morning,' the woman said with a warm smile when she reached them. Oscar hovered shyly behind her. 'We thought we'd bring you a little welcome.'

The delicious scent of fresh scones,

coffee cake, and fruit loaf, all piled high on her and Oscar's trays, floated across the garden like a mermaid's song.

'I'm Claudette, I work at the Barn,' she said, extending a brisk hand to Daniel, one of the actors.

'You're an angel,' Daniel said in awe, taking it and kissing it.

'Tsk, away with you,' she said, impatient with his theatricality, but amused too. Or maybe tickled by Daniel's beard. They made a picnic blanket out of jumpers and set about the feast.

Lizzie took a piece of fruit loaf from the tray Oscar had carried.

'Hello again,' she said to him.

He was hovering at the edge of the group and gave her an uncertain smile. She noticed he'd caught the sun on his face since the last time she saw him, which gave him a glow. He looked healthier.

'Are you going to put up a stage?' he asked, glancing around.

'Right here.' She measured out the space with gestures. 'Our carpenter hasn't arrived yet. You can help, if you like. We need all the help we can get.'

'I don't know . . . I'll ask . . . '

'My God, Lizzie, have you tasted this coffee cake?' Meredith joined them, ripping a chunk off her cake and handing it to Lizzie. 'I had to bring you some.'

Lizzie took it, her fingers sinking into the rich butter icing.

'This is my sister, Meredith,' she said to Oscar. 'And I'm Lizzie. You're Oscar, aren't you?'

He nodded, looking enquiringly at Meredith, who was licking the butter off her fingers, as if she was familiar to him. She gave him a wink. She was used to this particular stare from children.

'Do you listen to the Bedtime Stories on the Children's Channel?' Lizzie said, helping him out of his confusion.

Recognition dawned on his face, then excitement. Meredith's voice, given to a soft blue puppet bear, was part of the bedtime routine of thousands of children all over the country. It was Meredith's most stable source of work. Kids loved her. Parents loved her even more. Off to bed now, she said, and off the little ones went, obeying the gentle, husky voice, as reassuring as hot milk and honey.

Oscar quickly masked his excitement.

'I used to,' he said, lifting one shoulder in nonchalance. 'When I was little.'

'Yes,' Meredith said, appraising him. 'I can see you would have grown out of it. But maybe you could still put it on once in a while? Just so my boss thinks I'm doing a good job.'

'Ok,' Oscar said seriously. 'If you think it'd help.'

'After all, no one really grows out of stories, do they? Do you live here, little man?'

He nodded, a proud smile just tickling at the edge of his mouth.

'Lucky you.'

Lizzie might be able to put the stranger out of her mind, but she couldn't help falling for his son.

3

As she fell, Lizzie heard someone gasp. But even though she hit the grass quite heavily, after skipping completely the last four rungs of the ladder she'd been descending, it was embarrassment she felt more than any real hurt. Especially when the ladder fell sideways with a crash too.

'Lizzie! Are you ok?' Fatima asked, hurrying out of the summerhouse.

'Um . . . 'Lizzie raised herself up, shocked by the suddenness of the fall, the wind knocked out of her. She laughed bashfully, feeling like an idiot. 'I'm fine. My foot just slipped off the rung.'

'You're sure?' Now Kate was beside Fatima, the two of them still carrying the costumes they'd been in the middle of unpacking in the summerhouse while Lizzie — foolishly — had been clamouring over the roof looking for the best way to rig up spotlights.

'I'm fine,' Lizzie said again with a querulous smile. She brushed down her shorts with her stinging hands.

'You should have had someone holding the ladder,' Fatima scolded.

Lizzie's shame still outweighed her pain, so it was a surprise to see a thick drop of blood oozing from a graze on her knee.

She blinked, her teeth sinking into her bottom lip, and reached out a hand to the tree trunk beside her. When she looked up again there were black dots in front of her eyes, and more people around, all drawn by the commotion.

One was the man she'd seen with Oscar.

He was with a woman in a long flowery skirt, who wore a shoulder bag stuffed to bursting with files and papers; and next to him was someone else, someone Lizzie hadn't met yet, dressed in one of the costumes from the summerhouse. They all looked at her with concern.

Under the midday sun and all the

attention she was so hot suddenly that she could barely breathe.

'Are you hurt?' the man asked her.

'You're shaking,' noted the woman he was with.

She knew she'd turned pale. The woman in the costume watched her with interest, as if she was some great curiosity. Lizzie tried a long, slow breath, but already the world was becoming white and hazy at the edges and she couldn't speak.

Oh no, she thought, knowing exactly what was going to happen. She could feel it coming. Not in front of everyone!

She put all her will into resisting the faint, even pinching her thigh hard, but it was like resisting the pull of the tide. She felt herself sinking.

The man's voice sounded as if she were hearing it from under a blanket.

'I've got you,' he said. She felt his arms come around her, catching her.

★ ★ ★

Lizzie had known that today was going to be a significant day when she woke up and found a sixpence in her slipper.

Her grandmother used to leave them for her on the first day of school, for luck. New challenges, new opportunities, met with silver in your pocket. They were the exact same coins Lizzie's great-grandmother used to leave for Lizzie's grandmother — dozens of wished-on sixpences passed down through the generations.

Lizzie's grandmother had died nine years ago, but the coins kept appearing, filling Lizzie with anticipation every time she found one, reminding her the day was full of promise.

Meredith always pointed out it was more likely a sixpence had simply dropped free from the collection on Lizzie's dressing table. Lizzie didn't care about Meredith's teasing; she'd rather believe the coins came from their grandmother. After all, she'd always felt that her grandmother was still around.

★ ★ ★

She had originally gone up on the ladder to see if she could fix some lights, but when she discovered she could move about on the roof quite safely behind the heads of the decorative columns, she couldn't resist. There was access to the roof, she found, from the raised bank behind the summerhouse, and old flowerpots even suggested that someone had once built something of a garden up there.

The view was breath-taking. She could see right across the estate: the white façade of the Georgian house glowed with aged light, its great chimneystacks rising up in perfect symmetry. She could see across the avenue lined with lime trees, and the small classical folly half hidden in a copse.

In the far distance horses and cows grazed in the meadow, and behind her the sea glinted under the blue sky.

While she was pushing aside a heavy plant pot, she found some loose stonework. She dug her fingers into it and away came the largest stone, revealing a recess. Inside was a Victorian biscuit tin, decorated with sparrows and primroses.

Hidden treasure!

Eagerly, but with great care, she drew out the tin. It was difficult to get the lid off, but not as hard as she'd expected. Her heart pounding, she peered inside.

On the top was a small piece of aged red felt, crumpled and stiff, but there was nothing within its folds. Lizzie put it aside and found a stack of cream note-paper underneath.

The pages were browning and spotted with damp, and the ink of the elegant handwriting fading in many places. Even as she held the first letter it began to disintegrate along its creases.

It felt disrespectful suddenly, to risk destroying these letters. They didn't belong to her, she had no right to pry into their contents when their owner had so clearly wanted them kept private.

Lizzie's conscience was so pricked that she had the strange sensation she was being watched. It was so strong that she glanced back over her shoulder to check she was still alone.

The last thing in the tin was a photograph. It was stuck to the bottom; Lizzie had to needle it out. Although the image was faded at the edges, you could still see the figure of the straight-backed, smiling young man in uniform.

Love letters, Lizzie thought.

Again, she felt as though there were someone close at her shoulder and, humbled by the powerful emotional life of the items she'd discovered, she put them back just as she'd found them.

She stood up, again glancing around to see whether there was in fact anyone who had seen her. No one. But then she saw the man who'd been on her mind so much, walking on the lawn with a woman. What was it about him that touched her imagination so?

What Lizzie loved most in the world was a story, and just as the tin of letters had excited her with its promise of secrets and history, so, it seemed, did everything about Hartley. Even its residents.

★ ★ ★

Lizzie hadn't quite blacked out, but she felt very far away from the world. There was barely any sensation in her limbs but she was aware of the man taking her weight, almost lifting her. Now she couldn't tell if it was the sight of blood or mortification that was making her woozy.

'I've got a first aid kit in the house,' he said.

'I'll leave you to it,' the woman said. 'I hope you feel better, sweetie.' She touched Lizzie's arm. Lizzie wished she was gathered enough to thank her.

The man guided Lizzie over the grass and gravel towards Hartley House. When they crossed the threshold, the cool shade was an immediate relief, and she began to get her senses back. She was grateful to him for understanding what she needed most was a quiet place to sit.

She became aware of his arm around her waist, the warm sheen of moisture between his skin and hers.

'Really, you don't have to . . . 'she managed to say. But at the same time, she was leaning on the strength of his arm, unable to help herself.

Her face was turned to the soft material at his shoulder. He smelled of summer, of sunshine and cut grass and some faint lemony aftershave.

The pleasure-pain of the situation made her head reel.

She held on to him through the swaying rhythm of the climb up the stairs, hoping her weight wasn't a burden to him. She wondered if he could feel her heart pounding.

He helped her into his apartment, to a light, cosy living room, and set her down on the sofa. For a second his arm was trapped beneath her, and his gaze collided with hers, his face only inches away.

He carefully untangled himself.

'Oh!' Lizzie tried to sit up, to help him.

'Lie back,' he insisted. 'You've had a shock.'

She did as he said, only repositioning her legs to hang off the edge of the sofa, ashamed of her trainers on the cushions. When he went around the breakfast bar into the kitchen, she covered her face with her hands.

'It's embarrassing,' she mumbled.

'What is?' The tap was running. He turned from the sink to take a tin down from the cupboard.

'Fainting at the sight of blood. Like some wimpy Victorian heroine.'

And doing it in front of you, she wanted to add.

'It's a medical condition. There's a technical name for it I don't remember,' he said. 'It's nothing to be embarrassed about.'

He knelt beside her and held a cold cloth to her forehead with a clinical manner. She watched as he took some cotton wool and antiseptic out of the tin.

'Don't look, now,' he said.

She sucked air through her teeth at the

sting of the antiseptic on her torn knee.

Then, beautifully, the sting was taken away when he lightly blew on the graze.

The tender gesture moved her. She looked at his bent head, the soft black hair.

'How are your hands?' he said.

'Just bruised.'

'Let me see.'

She laid her hands in his, palms up. His thumbs moved over the tender heels of her hands where there were tiny cuts. He wiped an antiseptic pad across one, then the other.

'Not too bad,' he said.

Lizzie didn't want him to let go.

He went back into the tin for a plaster and applied it to her knee, his fingertips whispering against her skin. 'There you go.'

Finally, it was safe to look. She was appalled. She stared at the tiny plaster mournfully. 'You didn't have anything bigger? Just for the sake of my ego.'

One corner of his mouth lifted. It was almost a smile.

'I think that fall was dramatic enough to satisfy your ego.'

She smiled back at him, bashful but not quite so mortified any more, he was being so kind.

'I'm Lizzie,' she said eventually.

'Griffin. Griff.' He sat back on his heels. 'Can you sit up and drink some tea?'

'I'm sure I can. I feel much better. Thank you.'

'Or brandy, if you like.'

'Tea's fine.'

While he was in the kitchen, she gazed with interest around the room. She'd be happy to stay here all afternoon.

Against the wall to her right was a squat, wide bookcase, crammed full of books. Everything from airport thrillers to science books. They all looked read, their spines creased, their edges battered. He came back from the kitchen with a mug of tea and a Jammy Dodger in the shape of a smiley face.

'Oscar keeps telling me it's time I grew up and graduated to Jaffa Cakes,' he deadpanned.

She laughed. 'A well-stocked First Aid kit and a well-stocked biscuit tin,' she noted. 'Surely everything you need to be a good dad.'

He made a wincing smile, like she'd stepped on his foot and he was too polite to say anything.

'I'm not Oscar's dad. I'm looking after him for his mother. It's a private fostering arrangement.'

'I'm sorry, I didn't mean to be nosy . . . '

'You weren't. I thought you should know, since he seems to want to spend a lot of time with you all down in the garden.'

'We like his company. He's adorable.'

He looked at her with an expression she couldn't place.

'He hasn't been with me very long. That woman outside . . . ' He paused.

Lizzie blushed scarlet. Had he seen her watching them?

'She's a social worker. She was checking Oscar's staying in a suitable environment.'

'I can't imagine any environment better than this.'

'No,' Griff said softly. He was quiet a moment, then said, 'I used to live here with my mother.'

'At Oscar's age?'

'A bit older. On and off until I was nineteen.'

'The teenage years. There must be a lot of intense memories for you here,' she said. He fell quiet again.

'My sister Meredith — she's the director of our play — and me,' she said, offering something into the silence, 'we used to put on plays in the summer when we were kids, in our back garden.'

'Did you get big audiences?'

'My grandmother used to bring all her bingo friends. They'd sit and eat Fruit Pastels and cheer in all the right places. Then, when Meredith was thirteen, we fell out because her dressing room — that's what she called the Wendy house — took up all the space in the garden. That was the last time we worked together.'

'Until now.'

'Until now. Now she has the entire summerhouse for a dressing room,' she laughed.

He laughed too, and Lizzie tried not to stare at the lovely change it made to his serious face.

'Oscar told me about her,' he said. 'He's been very excited about meeting her.'

Lizzie chuckled. 'Yes. She has that effect on men.'

They were interrupted by shouting outside the door.

'Lizzie? Are you in there? Lizzie!'

Meredith, in a furious temper, appeared at the threshold.

'In here, Meredith,' Lizzie called. She mouthed to Griff, *sorry*.

Meredith marched in. 'Are you all right?'

'I'm fine. It's just a graze — '

'Because Fatima came and told me you'd gone into the house, semi-conscious, with a complete stranger.'

'Meredith,' Lizzie said, 'this is Griff — '

39

'Like a total idiot,' her sister went on.

'He's standing right beside you, Mer.'

Meredith turned and fixed her fierce glare on
Griff. 'He could be a psychopath. An axe murderer.' Lizzie winced. She hoped Griff would understand Meredith was just being an over-protective big sister.

'Not an axe murderer,' he said. 'Just occasionally thoughtless.' He offered his hand to Meredith. 'Also, I run The Barn restaurant. I'm sorry, I thought you knew.'

'Oh — the cakes were from you!' Lizzie said.

Meredith eyed him suspiciously but eventually shook his hand.

'My sister, the drama queen,' Lizzie said.

'No, she's right,' Griff said. 'Can you help Lizzie out, Meredith? She might be a bit shaky still.'

Lizzie was sorry to leave. 'I'm fine.' She stood up. 'And thank you,' she said, earnestly.

'Are you really all right?' Meredith asked as they headed back to the summerhouse.

'I'm fine. He took very good care of me.'

Meredith's concern was replaced by a knowing smile. Lizzie tried not to blush.

'It was embarrassing, though,' she said, 'in front of everyone. Who's the new girl I saw with Fatima and Kate?'

Meredith was puzzled. 'I can't think who that was. I'm sure you've met everyone.' She stopped as they reached the summerhouse, and gave Lizzie a hug. 'No more incidents or injuries, ok? I need you to look after yourself. You're important.'

'I'll do my best.'

She stood beside Lizzie and took a long look at the spot where the stage would be.

'Waverley was telling me they've put plays on in this exact spot for generations,' she said. 'Imagine that!'

41

'Really?' Lizzie was intrigued.

Meredith laughed. 'I knew that would make you happy. His grandmother used to put on performances with her friends during house parties. Look — he gave me photographs.'

She drew out a stack of small, sepia prints. 'Be careful with these, Calamity Jane. He wants them back.'

'Of course,' Lizzie murmured. She barely noticed as Meredith left her, she was too absorbed in the images of Hartley a hundred years ago, the unsmiling men in waistcoats and women with full skirts.

In particular she was mesmerised by one young freckled face beneath a white parasol, her chin tilted with entitlement and attitude. The same girl — in the same white dress — Lizzie had seen earlier, who had peered at her with such curiosity.

Lizzie flipped the photo over. Victoria Grey, Summer 1899.

She raised her eyes from the pictures dazedly.

She was alone. Through the windows of the summerhouse she could see costumes hung along the picture rail like headless bodies. The world felt upended. A cloud passed over the sun and Lizzie stopped beside the ladder, which was still on the ground where it had fallen. On the earth beside it she saw three dried drops of blood.

4

Griff tidied up in the living room, helping himself to a biscuit, and then left the house too. He had to get back to the restaurant. Tonight's menu: watercress and courgette soup, squash ravioli pork loins in blackcurrant wine.

Thank goodness for Claudette. Not only was she a fantastic chef, but since she was a mum herself, they could work together to make their professional lives as family-friendly as possible, covering for each other as needed.

Who would have thought there would be a silver lining to his old chef and partner having been embezzling funds for eighteen months, almost bankrupting them? The anger and sense of betrayal still made Griff's teeth grind and his nights sleepless, but things were getting back on track with this new venture.

Great staff and loyal customers helped. The ideal he still held on to, of creating a place warm and welcoming, unpretentious and nourishing, was a dream he refused to let go of. And it was hard to argue that things hadn't turned out for the best when being at Hartley House was obviously so good for Oscar.

That didn't mean conversations with his accountant were any fun yet. Or that he didn't have a million things to worry about.

On his way back to the barn he found Oscar outside, holding a bag for Waverley as he deadheaded the roses.

'Want to come for a walk with me, O?' Oscar put down the bag. Then he scooped it up again. 'Is that ok?' he asked Waverley.

Waverley nodded. 'I've nearly finished here.'

Oscar dropped the bag and raced over to Griff.

The two of them walked through the garden in companionable silence. Clouds drifted over the sun in that changeable English summertime way as they went past the empty stables and the old donkey garden.

Griff stretched his shoulders, feeling an ache there, and in his arms and back and chest, from the familiarity of each scene. There were memories everywhere.

Eventually they came to the pear tree. They both stopped. Griff looked at Oscar. Oscar looked back at him.

He knew too.

The tree was under Oscar's window now, just as it used to be under Griff's when that room was his. Griff had called it his escape tree. One solid branch reached its fingers right up to the glass. It hadn't grown like other trees; he was sure he'd wished it into existence.

He used to use it to go and see Mia.

'Have you heard from your mum, Oscar?'

'Not since she phoned last week.'

He didn't elaborate. Griff understood. It was complicated for the poor kid.

Living with Mia was hard. You never knew what kind of mood she'd be in, whether a conversation with her would elate you or wring you out. That didn't mean Oscar didn't miss her. He loved her.

And Mia loved him too, Griff knew.

He rested his hand on the crown of Oscar's head atop his silky, fine hair.

What more can I do? he thought. *The problem is, we're both too serious.*

Oscar moved slightly towards him, until he was against Griff's side, and Griff dropped his hand onto Oscar's shoulder.

We need a Lizzie, he thought, briefly, before he could censor himself.

Her face popped into his mind: her fair, translucent skin, those laughing grey eyes, so open and full of hope, as if expecting great things to happen any minute. Her dark blond hair was mussed, the ends just long enough to curl under her naked earlobes. In a plain shirt and shorts she'd looked unfussy, uncomplicated, and the fresh-faced earnestness of her hit him somewhere under the ribs, like a warm hand reaching in to take hold of his insides. There you are, he had thought, out of nowhere, when she looked up at him from the crook of his arm.

Stupid, really. Mad romanticism from someone who wasn't a romantic at all.

It was a relief when her sister came in to give him a hard time in a voice like liquorice whips.

With a sigh he rubbed a hand over his face and checked his watch. Later he had to meet one of his suppliers, see if he could squeeze a few weeks of credit out of them.

He had too much going on in his life right now. There was no sane person in the world who would want to be part of it. And Griff knew what it was like to have your heart played with. He wouldn't risk doing it to someone else.

5

Lizzie sat on the grass with her laptop, updating the theatre company's website and checking on their ticket sales (a slow start, but picking up), and trying not to scratch the scab on her knee. At the same time, she watched Meredith take the cast through the rehearsal of the scene where Alice meets the Cheshire Cat.

She couldn't help beaming with pride. Her sister was so good at this: inspiring, authoritative and insightful. Daniel, Kate and Fatima were all listening attentively.

But then something odd happened. Jerome, the carpenter who was helping them with set building, walked behind the rehearsal group, wearing his toolbelt and carrying a plank of wood on his broad shoulders. Lizzie saw Meredith notice him, she saw Meredith's gaze follow him as he passed. She saw Meredith's train of thought become thoroughly derailed and the words dry up on her tongue.

Even her hands froze in mid expression.

'Um,' Meredith said after a brief pause. 'Let's just try that, then, shall we?' And she stepped back and waved to indicate that they others should carry on with the scene.

To Lizzie, it seemed as though Meredith were trying really hard not to look at Jerome as he went about his work, and she watched her sister's discomfort with a certain kind of glee.

It was about time Meredith found someone who could do that to her for a change.

Interesting, too, that it should be Jerome. He was older than her, with grey mixed in his dark blond hair, and was certainly a man of few words.

Lizzie had heard so little from him when they'd discussed the project she couldn't even decode if his accent was Yorkshire or Scottish.

'Afternoon!' Waverley called, approaching Lizzie across the grass. 'I heard about your fall the other day. Are you all right?'

He sat down beside her, crossing his legs, crushing a crowd of daisies under the seat of his chinos and looping his elbows around his knees. She saw he had bumblebees on his socks, and grinned at him, liking him so much that she wasn't even embarrassed to be reminded of her clumsiness.

'I'm fine. It was nothing.'

'Glad to hear it. We've been on an upward trend recently here at Hartley and I'd hate for any gruesome injuries to spoil it.'

'I hope we'll be part of your upward trend,' Lizzie said.

'I don't doubt it. It's wonderful to have you all here.' He exhaled happily as he watched Oscar run across the sunlit grass to give Meredith something he'd fetched for her. There was perfect contentment on Oscar's face when Meredith put her hand on his shoulder to keep him beside her to watch the rehearsal.

'We had a bit of a dark patch for a while,' Waverley said. 'The estate has had some misfortune since the time Griff

51

lived here. I wasn't sure we'd even be able to keep hold of it. But then Griff came back, with Oscar. The gorgeousness of the two of them! Don't you think?'

'Oh. Yes,' she said, taking her cue. But it wasn't hard to agree.

'And from that moment things started turning around. And then you, of course.' He smiled at her again.

'I think perhaps it has more to do with your hard work and kindness than our showing up,' Lizzie said.

'I don't know. It feels more like the universe has been put back on its right course somehow.'

Lizzie didn't answer. To her, it did feel like fate that they were here. But she was sentimental like that; she hadn't expected the same from Waverley.

'I'd love to know more about the history of the house,' she said, closing her laptop and turning to him more fully. 'I was wondering if I could perhaps use your library? But I don't want to intrude . . . '

'Of course you can. With pleasure.'

'Those photos of your grandmother

were so interesting.'

'She was very interesting, my grandmother. I'll leave a few things out for you, if you like. Just come on in whenever you fancy. The house knows you now, it'll be welcoming.'

Lizzie hesitated a moment, unsure how to take that comment, but then laughed. Well, why shouldn't the house have a character? It certainly had personality.

Impulsively, she said, 'Meredith was wondering whether you had any ghosts . . . ?'

She expected Waverley to laugh too, but he responded as if it was a perfectly rational question.

'You would think so, a house of this age, wouldn't you?' He rubbed his chin. 'My sister saw a ghost once.'

He glanced at Lizzie, watched her face. Then he shot a quick smile. 'But she was pregnant and heat-stroked at the time.'

He put his legs straight in front of him, made windshield wipers with his feet to stretch his ankles.

'Wouldn't it be fun to set up a haunted tour for Halloween, though?' he said.

Lizzie let her hands fall down into the grass and tried to resist the urge to pick at the plaster on her knee. Of course he was joking. No one rational believed in ghosts.

'By the way,' Waverley said, 'what are you all doing tomorrow evening?'

6

'I think we've got a poltergeist,' Fatima said. Daniel and Meredith chuckled, but Lizzie didn't. 'No, seriously,' Fatima insisted. 'How else do you explain everything going missing?'

'Being scatter-brained?' Daniel suggested. He pinched a sausage roll from the plate in front of him and Fatima slapped his hand in admonishment — a little harder than she probably needed to.

'You can't start eating until the birthday boy gets here.'

Daniel rolled his eyes. It felt quite odd, Lizzie had to admit, to be in a group of adults dressed in yellow and crimson Gryffindor scarves, standing at a table of pastries shaped like sorting hats and magic wands, in a restaurant decorated with owls, toads and broomsticks . . . but she suspected she wasn't the only one secretly delighted by it. Griff had done a great job. She'd have been thrilled to have a party like this for her eighth birthday.

'I think the Harry Potter theme is going to your head,' Daniel teased Fatima. 'You're thinking of the poltergeist from Hogwarts.'

'Neither of us is careless with the props,' Kate said, coming to Fatima's defence. 'But things keep moving around. Everything was disordered in the summerhouse this morning. And I can't find the Queen of Hearts' necklace anywhere — you know, the one with the cameo and rubies? It's only costume jewellery, but still . . .'

'And my phone charger vanished out of my bag,' Fatima added. She paused. 'I think it was in my bag . . .'

'No, you're right, a ghost is the only logical explanation,' Daniel laughed.

Lizzie was listening but not contributing to the conversation. Her gaze kept being pulled to Griff, who was on the opposite side of the restaurant putting the last touches to giant cardboard dragon. Claudette, the chef, was with him, and beside her, her daughter, who was about the same age as Oscar, with thick blond hair plated in an intricate design around the crown of her head. She wore shorts and scuffed trainers and when she caught Lizzie's eye, she gave her a cheery gap-toothed grin.

There weren't any other children at the party. It confirmed the impression Lizzie had got from Oscar that he either hadn't had the chance to make any friends at his new school, or his natural reserve meant that he found it hard to do so.

Griff's gaze followed the little girl's, and when he saw Lizzie, he smiled at her also. Lizzie's whole body lit up, until she found she was practically on her toes, and she had to take herself in hand, turning back to her friends.

She tuned into what Kate was saying: 'It'll probably turn up.'

Daniel hushed them, gesturing to the door of the restaurant as it opened. He leapt to the front of the group, a party popper in his hand. As everyone yelled 'Surprise!' Daniel let off the popper, sending showers of paper curls over Oscar, and over Waverley too, who was a step behind Oscar.

Oscar was startled, and blushed. But then his gaze found Griff, who gave him an encouraging nod, as if to confirm, No, this really is for you. And Oscar's expression turned to pure joy.

Daniel began a rendition of *Happy Birthday* in his best opera voice as Waverley guided Oscar gently forward. But lovely though Oscar's reaction was, it was Griff's face as he watched the little boy that Lizzie couldn't take her eyes off.

★　★　★

After presents, and cutting the cake, they all went outside for a game of Quidditch. However, the broomsticks became something of a tripping hazard (especially to the adults who'd started on the champagne), so it gradually turned into a game of rounders instead.

Oscar didn't mind. He was a fantastically speedy runner and seemed to be scoring all the points. Between his speed and little Laurel's amazing bowling skills, they were trouncing the adults.

'That looks like the beginning of a beautiful friendship,' Lizzie remarked to Griff when she saw Claudette's daughter and Oscar high-five each other after getting Griff 'out' on the third post.

Griff was bent over, hands on his knees, wheezing. He'd really done his best to outrun them.

'You're a bit competitive, aren't you?' she asked with amusement. She'd already had her turn at batting and had failed, three times, to hit the ball. It reminded her of school sports days, and she was doing now what she'd usually ended up doing then: sitting on the grass making daisy chains, watching everyone else argue over the score.

It was pleasurable, watching the cool summer evening slowly come on, the light growing dimpsy, lamps going on in the windows of the house. A couple of the other tenants had come down to join the game; a few more spectated from windows, cheering when Oscar got a rounder.

Griff straightened up, holding his side, wincing.

'I used to be good at rounders. I'm not that old. How did this happen?'

Lizzie laughed. 'You're out of practice.'

Daniel had roped in Jerome to play on his team, and Jerome stepped up for his turn, flexing his hands around the wooden bat. Claudette bowled, and Jerome struck the ball so heartily that it flew right over Lizzie's head and all the way into the old stable block.

'I'll get it!' Griff called, raising his hand. 'You can use the quaffle in the meantime!'

He tilted his head at Lizzie. 'Want to give me a hand?'

She leapt up at the invitation and followed him towards the stables. He had a grass stain under the bottom pocket of his jeans and his tee shirt hung wonky at his shoulder, and when he glanced back at her she thought how relaxed and contented he looked.

'It's been a great afternoon,' she said, hopping forward a step to enter the stables beside him.

'I'm glad. I hope Oscar enjoyed it.'

'He seems to be having a brilliant time.'

'Thanks to you all for coming.'

Lizzie paused to let her eyes adjust to the dusky interior of the stable block. The stalls were empty, only the posts were left standing, and old dry straw and hay was strewn across the floor. It still had that smell, musty and leathery, with a not unpleasant tang of manure, and she imagined where the tack had hung and where the grooms sat to drink their tea.

'It's like going back a hundred years,' she said.

Griff gazed around, as if seeing it through her eyes.

'A hundred years ago feels much nearer in this house,' he said. 'Sometimes it's as if nothing separates us at all.'

He began to hunt for the small rounders ball.

'I had a couple of birthdays here at Hartley,' he said as he kicked aside a mound of straw gathered in the corner. 'Not in the summer, though; my birthday's in January. When I was sixteen Waverley arranged a wassailing party around the old apple tree in the meadow, with a bonfire and music. I was allowed to drink cider; my mum got quite tipsy on it. So did Mia. Oscar's mum.'

'Maybe Waverley should go into event planning,' Lizzie said, smiling. 'It seems like he's got a talent for it.' She rounded one of the posts. 'Did Mia live here too, then?' She'd been wondering about Oscar's mum but didn't want to be nosy.

'No, she lived in town. We were neighbours, until my dad left and my mum got a job in Waverley's housekeeping team. Mum and I moved in so she could be on site. And then, when she died, Waverley let me stay on until I went to university. Which I never would have got into without him.' He paused in checking the ground, and said in a careful voice, 'It sort of felt like he adopted me.'

Lizzie, who knew what it was like to lose parents young, didn't say anything, but stepped absent-mindedly onto a rotten wooden beam that had fallen across the floor. As she did so, she somehow lost her balance, and then lost her footing, and fell back off the beam and almost tumbled over, just missing scraping her shin on the concrete.

Embarrassed, she looked at Griff and was relieved to see that he had his back to her and hadn't noticed. He's going to think I'm so graceless and clumsy!

She wasn't usually so awkward. She didn't even know how it had happened; it had felt like the beam had moved out from under her.

Concentrate! she told herself, wiping her palms on her shorts.

'Things were different in those days,' Griff went on. 'Waverley only had to open the house up a few times a year. The estate was starting to do well before

I left. I'm not sure what happened really, just a succession of small things: less income from the land tenants, tax issues, dry rot in the roof . . . you know how things can be.'

'Waverley told me that having you and Oscar in the house put the universe back in order.'

'If only!' He shook his head. 'The universe doesn't feel so tidy right now.'

But Lizzie, marvelling at the fact that she was standing here alone with him, while outside she could hear the laughter of her friends at a party for someone she hadn't even known a week ago . . . she had to wonder whether in fact Waverley had a point. Some things, she knew, were beyond explanation.

The mystery of it seemed especially present then, she felt, and Griff seemed to read something of it in her face, because in the low shadowed light their eyes met, and they drank each other in.

He feels it too, she thought.

She was falling at Griff's feet.

Literally. The ground rushed towards

her; she barely had time to put her hands out to try to break her fall.

She was jarred against Griff's shoulder as he somehow reached her quickly enough to catch her and she thudded into him.

'Whoops!' He caught her with his arm braced under her shoulder and tried to help her up. Lizzie noticed something half hidden in the dry straw where she had almost landed her hands, and once she was upright she toed the straw aside to reveal the upward prong of a bent, rusted nail, the kind that may have come loose from a horseshoe.

Griff stared at it too. It could have caused a very nasty injury. His face turned pale.

'Are you all right?' he asked.

She couldn't answer. Griff picked up the nail and threw it into the far corner. 'I'll speak to Waverley about having this place cleaned . . . ' Turning back to her, he tried to lighten the mood. 'Are you going to make a habit of this?'

She just looked at him. How could she

tell him? It wasn't in her nature to keep secrets, but how could she say, 'Listen, no, I'm not clumsy — I was pushed.'

She'd felt the nudge behind her leg, as sharp as a kick, buckling her knee. Aiming her towards that hidden nail.

But of course there was no one behind her. No one but the two of them in the stables.

All of Lizzie's life, Meredith had teased her for her imagination. Her teachers, her grandmother, had made excuses for it. Poor Lizzie. Her way of coping . . .

Others were less kind, and had different words for it.

Griff was already looking at her with concern, and a little dismay.

'Sorry.' She forced a smile, putting a hand over her hammering heart. 'I'm an idiot. Let's go back.'

He started to say something, but Lizzie was already heading out of the stables. Outside, the sky was losing its light and the rounders game had been reduced to Daniel and Meredith playing Catch while everyone else returned to pick at the cake. Lizzie half turned back to Griff, avoiding his eyes.

'I have to go and finish some work before tomorrow...'

'Lizzie, have I done something?'

'Thanks for a nice evening.'

They had spoken at the same time, so she was able to pretend she hadn't heard him, though they both knew she had.

She started off across the lawn, towards the summerhouse. She didn't look back. She felt too embarrassed.

What had happened, though? What had actually happened?

Maybe she had stumbled. Maybe she had imagined the shove.

But no. No matter how many others doubted Lizzie, she never doubted herself. She knew where the line was between her imagination and real life. And she knew there was something in this house that wished her harm.

★ ★ ★

The grounds of the summerhouse were empty as Lizzie approached the building to retrieve her folders of notes, but there was a small light coming from inside that at first made her think Kate had left something on. But as Lizzie came closer, she saw the light brighten and shrink in the window. She froze, watching.

Who could be in there? No one: they were all still at the party.

She kept watching: the ethereal bluish light didn't flicker but shone steadily now. She put her hand to the back of her neck. It was prickling, as though someone were watching her. She glanced around. There was no one that she could see, but the trees made good hiding places.

'This is ridiculous,' she muttered, cross with herself for the weakness in her knees. She strode forward, opening the door into the summerhouse and entering fully inside, like a parent throwing open the wardrobe doors to convince a child there were no monsters. But it was herself she was trying to convince.

The light was coming from the corner

where they had the props table. Lizzie went towards it, recognising something familiar about the glow. But the time she reached it, relief was loosening her tense muscles and she was ready to laugh at herself: it was the lit screen of a mobile phone, plugged into a charger.

Probably Fatima's lost charger turned up, Lizzie thought, and she flicked on the overhead bulb.

The sudden light illuminated the figure standing silently behind the rail of costumes, and Lizzie let out a shriek.

7

Griff was in the closed restaurant the next morning, packing away dragons' eggs and broomsticks and wondering what on earth to do with them now, when the door opened and Lizzie stopped on the threshold. 'Hi, have you got a minute?' 'Of course!' He tried to wipe the glitter off his hands. 'Come in.'

After the strange way they'd parted yesterday he hadn't been able to decide whether to go and find her, so he was glad she was here. She was dressed for the overcast day in a cardigan the colour of strawberries, and anxiously fiddled with the cuffs of the sleeves as she joined him.

She smiled uncertainly. 'Are we on our own?'

'A couple of the cooks are in the kitchen.' He frowned slightly, intrigued. Something about her manner suggested she was about to tell secrets. 'Is everything ok?'

She took a breath, letting her hand drop to steeple her fingertips on the table between them. He wondered if he should speak first. But maybe he'd talked too much already, and maybe that was why she'd left so suddenly yesterday; maybe, being so unused to opening up, he'd misjudged and shared too much. He kept quiet and waited for Lizzie to say what she'd come here to say.

'I went back to the summerhouse after I left you yesterday,' she said. Her cheeks were pink. She looked so uncomfortable that he wished he could do something to reassure her that he wouldn't mind anything she said to him. 'And someone was in there.' She looked directly at him now, and said in a rush, 'It was Oscar's mum. She stayed there last night.'

Griff took a step back, floored. 'What?'

'She said she'd hoped to see Oscar on his birthday, but she was afraid to talk to him in front of everyone. She feels she's let him down recently and she was afraid he — or you — would be angry if she just turned up.'

Lizzie cleared her throat and looked away again, seeming full of apology for invading his privacy like this.

'I offered to let you know she was here,' Lizzie went on, 'but she seemed quite anxious . . .'

Griff could imagine. Mia, all keyed up with the drama of arriving uninvited.

'She made me promise to wait until this morning to speak to you,' Lizzie said. 'She didn't want to interrupt the party.'

'But why is she staying in the summer-house?' Griff asked, perplexed.

'I got the impression she might be in some trouble. She said she's going to be moving away for a while and she wanted to see Oscar before she left.'

Money trouble, relationship trouble, landlord trouble . . . Mia had had them all. Griff hoped she was healthy at least. He considered asking Lizzie how Mia looked, but didn't want to burden her by asking for her judgement. Mia had already asked too much; she'd obviously tried to play on Lizzie's sympathy.

'Of course I'm not angry,' Griff said, with a sigh. He sank into a chair. 'But I can't pretend it's not a disruption. Just as Oscar is getting settled.' It was hard to know how Oscar was going to respond to this.

He glanced up at Lizzie. 'Mia's complicated,' he said, 'but she'd not a bad person. She's always wanted the best for Oscar.'

Lizzie sat down with him. 'That's the impression I got,' she said generously.

He wondered if he'd ever find out now why Lizzie left yesterday. It was as if their relationship, new as it was, had been derailed somehow by the situation with Mia, and knocked off the hopeful path it had been on.

'I'm sorry you were dragged into this,' he said.

She smiled ruefully, and her hands came closer to his on the table. 'I just wish I could do more. I told her we could find somewhere better for her to stay but she insisted. I left the key with her. Maybe you could let Waverley know?

Will he mind?'

'I hope not.'

They sat in silence for a moment. He heard a seagull calling outside and the muted sounds from the cooks in the kitchen.

'So,' he said eventually, 'not a ghost, then?'

She looked startled, and then chuckled self-consciously, and drew back into herself. 'Oh, you mean Fatima's poltergeist? No. Of course not. No one believes in things like that.'

'I'm not so sure. Just because it's unlikely, doesn't mean it's impossible, right?'

Her smile was pure reward, but he wasn't sure what he'd done to deserve it. He was glad at least that he could let her leave looking happier than when she'd come in. But she didn't let her gaze linger on his.

'Mia said she would wait for you in the folly,' she said, standing up.

'Thanks, Lizzie.'

She paused, half turned. 'Should I

have stayed out of it?'

She was worried she'd intruded. Her sensitivity would make her draw back now.

Griff was angry at Mia, he realised. She shouldn't have used Lizzie like this.

'Mia really does need to start fighting her own battles,' he said, not able to hide his frustration.

★ ★ ★

It was half an hour before he could get away to meet Mia. The sky was white overhead and the air slightly muggy; a cloud of gnats flew into his face as he walked past the hydrangea at the entrance to the stone folly.

Mia was curled up in the curved windowsill at the far end. She dropped her feet to the ground when she saw him and rushed into his arms.

He returned the embrace. She'd been his first love, his best friend, the one who introduced him to so much of what life was. Mia had celebrated every teenage milestone with him. She was Oscar's mum. She remembered Griff's mother. They were intertwined. He loved her to pieces.

She exasperated him to death.

He put his hands on her shoulders and held her away from him.

'What's going on, Mia? Why all the subterfuge? Are you on the run?'

She gave him her charming, hopeless, can't-help-it grin. 'Kind of.'

He sighed and looked hard at her, still keeping her in his grip. She appeared healthy enough. She was slight, but didn't seem to have lost any weight that he could tell. There was colour in her cheeks and her long dark hair was neat and shining. Her ankle-length summer dress was clean. For the moment there was none of the fragility that sometimes came over her that he'd expected and dreaded to see.

He could imagine she'd played the victim for Lizzie, though.

'What about your job with the travel agent?' he asked.

She shrugged. 'They made some changes to their workforce.'

He raised an eyebrow. 'And sleeping in the summerhouse?'

'I just didn't want to make a fuss and be a burden. And I wanted to be sure Oscar wanted to see me . . . He was a bit upset with me the last time we spoke.' She pulled herself free of him. 'It's perfectly cosy in there, it's not like I was sleeping on a park bench or anything.'

'It's in use,' he reminded her.

'I noticed. There was lots of soft stuff to sleep on.' She grinned at him, and catching his hand, she walked backwards and drew him with her to sit on the window ledge together.

'So?' she said. 'How's my lovely boy?'

'Oscar's fine. He would have been happy to see you yesterday. You know he'd forgive you anything.'

Mia huffed defensively. 'I know. But it's better this way.'

'Why?'

She evaded his gaze. 'I'm just trying to keep things low-key, okay? There were a lot of strangers around yesterday. The fewer people who know that I'm here the better.'

So then: she was avoiding someone. Someone who might know to look for her at her son's birthday.

'Mia . . . ' Griff tried to gentle his voice and not show his frustration. 'If you're in trouble you need to tell me — '

'It's no big deal,' she said. 'You know I've got terrible taste in men.' She stuck her tongue out at him teasingly. 'It just means it's a good time for me to make a new start. I've got a friend in Manchester I can stay with. I wanted to see Oscar before I go. He is all right, isn't he?'

'He really is, Mia. He's happy here. But he misses you.'

Mia gripped Griff's hand and lifted his knuckles to her closed lips. 'I knew he'd be better off with you.'

Griff turned slightly, squeezing her fingers before taking his hand back.

'Do you need any money?' he asked.

'No.' She scowled at him as if offended, but it was unconvincing. 'I can take care of myself.'

'I'm glad to hear it.' He half smiled, and then stood up, smoothing down his tie. 'I need to get back to work.' From his pocket he took out his keys. 'Here: let yourself into the flat. Oscar's in the garden — I think he's learning how to build a stage this morning. I'll let him know you're here.'

He paused. A large stuffed rucksack was propped against the wall; did it hold everything she owned in the world?

'Help yourself to whatever's in the kitchen,' he said.

He turned, but turned back, adding with a stern, pointing finger, 'But nothing else.'

One of the many things Mia had introduced him to as a teenager was his first — and only — shoplifting experience.

She gave him the Scout salute.

Griff headed towards the summer-house, feeling some trepidation about breaking the news to Oscar that his mother was here. Griff would do what he could to help Mia, but Oscar always came first.

He found Oscar running around the half-finished stage, Laurel chasing him with a dripping paintbrush and both of them laughing, covered in paint colours. He hated to interrupt when Oscar seemed to be having so much fun.

No doubt he would be thrilled to see Mia, no matter how many complicated feelings it stirred up. But then, of course, there would have to come another goodbye.

8

As she crossed the lawn towards the main entrance of the house and stepped onto the driveway, Lizzie was aware of an ache at the top of her calf where a bruise had bloomed. But her mind was on other things.

I should have stayed out of it, she thought, I should have said sorry, but this is none of my business . . .

She kept picturing Griff's face when she came into the restaurant. He'd seemed so pleased to see her. The compliment of it rushed all the way through her like champagne.

But as soon as she mentioned Mia the champagne went flat. If Lizzie felt awkward about bringing up his complicated private business, it was clear that Griff was just as uncomfortable.

She was too soft, that was the problem. The girl in the summerhouse, with her large fawn coloured eyes and tear-spiked lashes, had tugged at Lizzie's heartstrings. Imagine having nowhere to sleep, and just wanting to see your child. Lizzie couldn't say no to her.

She didn't dwell on the fact that she was fairly sure that it was Fatima's charger that Mia was using, and that Mia's presence explained not just the disorder of their things the day before, but perhaps their disappearance too. She supposed it was her own fault for leaving the summerhouse unlocked.

Lizzie bit her fingertips thoughtfully. Where to go from here with Griff?

Space. She'd give him space.

The crunching beat of her footsteps on the gravel driveway had ceased some time ago, and she came out of her thoughts to realise she'd somehow walked straight past the entrance and was at the side of the house. She gazed around blankly. If she was orientating herself properly, the window above her looked out from Griff's flat. She stared up at it longingly. Then, with a sigh, she fell back against the tree that grew right up to his window.

The tree showered some white petals onto her shoulder, shaken loose from a blossom where the bud of a pear was beginning to show.

'Aren't you pretty?' she whispered, touching her hand to its wide, full trunk.

Lizzie Palmerstone, she told herself sternly, you don't have time for this. There's a company meeting in an hour and you're supposed to be in the library right now.

Having decided not to intrude on Griff's privacy any further, she was about to invade someone else's. It occurred to her that perhaps it was her disturbing Victoria's tin of letters that had made Victoria so angry with Lizzie, and that she wouldn't take kindly to any more poking about in her business. But if Victoria wasn't going to leave Lizzie alone, Lizzie had no choice but to try to find out more about the unquiet spirit.

She stirred herself and went back to the entrance. The main door to the house was open, so she went inside, and left it ajar behind her.

The first doorway on the left led to the library. A calm came over Lizzie as soon as she walked into the room. She loved full bookshelves; they were like an armour against the world. And Hartley's shelves, fitted along three of the Edwardian Blue painted walls, were stuffed with everything from elegant leather-bound classics to photo albums to what looked intriguingly like they might be handwritten journals.

A carved fireplace stood empty on one wall, and three worn leather armchairs were arranged around it. On a round table in front of the single window, Waverley was placing piles of folders and open books.

'Ah, Lizzie!' he saidin greeting.'You've started me off on something here! I've been all morning finding things I'd forgotten we had. Family history. I'm afraid I'm going to bore you to tears,' he said cheerfully.

Lizzie, who hadn't expected to see him, was nonetheless glad for the company. It put her in an awkward position, however: should she mention Mia? She decided to let Griff tell him about it, as they planned.

'This dear old room just gave me everything I thought you might be interested in,' Waverley went on. He brandished a stiff scrapbook at her. 'Look at this: my grandparents' wedding announcement.'

Lizzie left her heavy bag on a chair and came to stand at his shoulder. He spread the book on the table and pointed with a broad, flat fingernail at a newspaper cutting pasted inside.

'1903,' he said. 'Mr and Mrs Hubert Grey would like to announce . . . dum-de-dum . . . ' He hummed as he skimmed over the page. 'Miss Victoria Grey, to Mr Clifford Waverley of Waverley Tabaco.'

Lizzie peered at the photo of the couple beneath the text. They stood side by side, not touching, not smiling, as if being measured for their coffins.

'My grandfather wasn't exactly known for his light-heartedness,' Waverley said ruefully, reading Lizzie's mind. 'But by

Jove they knew how to grow a tash in those days, huh?'

Lizzie chuckled. Clifford certainly had an impressive moustache. It spanned the whole width of his face, wax-tipped to curving points.

'I don't think it was a love match,' Waverley went on. 'It was more to suit her parents than Victoria.' He looked musingly at the photo. 'She looks awfully like my mother here. But so young!'

'Was he ever in the armed forces, your grandfather?' Lizzie asked, thinking of the man in uniform she'd seen in the photo in the tin. She couldn't tell from the grainy print if this was the same person.

'Heavens, no. My grandmother might have liked him a bit more if he had been.'

Lizzie thought it was quite a sad way to talk about a relationship.

'Were they never happy together?'

'I'm sure they had their moments. But she died quite young, long before I came along. I never knew her. My other grandfather, my father's father, used to take me out fishing and tell me stories about when they were young together. He used to come to Hartley for summer parties and said how Victoria was so lovely she had all the young men after her. Could have had her pick, he said. And a little wild too, apparently. Though you wouldn't be able to tell from this picture, would you?'

He grinned at Lizzie. 'A real chatterbox, my granddad. Liked a drink too, so I'm not sure how accurate much of it was.' He squinted at her, clearly enjoying her interest. 'I'll let you in on a family secret, if you promise not to tell anyone.'

'Oh, I'm not sure . . . 'Lizzie said, stepping back.

She felt she was carrying enough secrets just now. 'It's all right, there's no one to be harmed by it.'

He bent to run his finger around the curved front of the table, as if to show off the smoothness of it. The varnished mahogany was slightly dulled by use. Then, sliding his finger under the desk, he made a motion and the front panel separated out, revealing a secret compartment.

'How ingenious!' Lizzie said. 'You'd never be able to guess there was an opening there.'

She leaned closer to look. Waverley closed the drawer again and she searched hard for the join but couldn't see it, not until he opened it up again. The drawer was shallow and small, with faint ink splatters inside.

'Victoria's father used to keep his . . . ahem . . . 'other' accounts book in here,' Waverley said. 'I'm ashamed to say our family had quite a thriving business with the local smugglers, going back generations. Our cove is the perfect landing spot.'

He didn't look ashamed; he was positively gleeful.

Lizzie found it fascinating too. 'Did they ever get caught?'

'Not a chance. Too many people in on it. Practically the whole local economy floated on it at one time.' He rocked back on his heels. 'It was all over when

Victoria inherited the house, though.'

'She was living here when she died, then?' Lizzie asked, lightly touching the corner of the scrapbook but superstitiously avoiding the eye of the woman in the photograph.

'Yes. Pneumonia, I believe. Early morning walks did for her. She wasn't very strong.'

Waverley turned back to the photo thoughtfully.

'She was tarnished, my grandfather said. That was the word he used. Odd one, isn't it? 'Tarnished' by an inappropriate liaison in her youth. Some scoundrel broke her heart and ruined her reputation. I suppose that was when her smile vanished.' He sighed. 'What a waste. Imagine what she might have done if she'd been allowed to be wild.'

Lizzie pictured Victoria as she'd seen her that day in the garden. She'd been fresh-faced, dressed in white summer dress. Not a matronly wife; not a woman bowed by disappointment. She'd been young. And that was the phase her spirit was stuck in.

She turned the pages of the scrapbook backwards and found more photos, playbills, dried flowers caught in the spine of the book after their glue came unstuck. Souvenirs of a life as it was lived.

Waverley had fallen silent, absorbed in a newspaper cutting that seemed to be about a ship returning from the West Indies. Lizzie glanced up. A drizzle was falling outside the window, obscuring the view of the garden, and on the mantle a carriage clock ticked loudly. Lizzie had the sense that the library was more crowded than it should be, as if someone had come in and was standing close behind her, waiting for someone to look up and notice her. Slowly, first from the corner of her eye, then directly, Lizzie glanced around the empty room.

I know you're there, she thought.

★ ★ ★

The hour passed quickly. Leaving Waverley engrossed in a stack of handwritten correspondence, Lizzie dashed across the wet lawn, her trainers squeaking, and broke into the summerhouse with water droplets on her eyelashes and hair.

'Don't panic,' Kate said, greeting her. 'It's supposed to clear up this afternoon and then we'll have fine weather right into opening night.'

Meredith snorted. 'Yes. And the weather forecast is never wrong.'

They were all crammed into the summerhouse with the props, scenery and equipment. Fatima was sitting on Daniel's lap, her flouncy skirt spread across their knees; Meredith had the second chair. Jerome was standing by the doorway as if desperate to be outside again, the bulk of him making the place seem even smaller and more cramped. And Laurel was perched on the table, swinging her legs, glancing hopefully out of the window every few moments.

Oscar, Lizzie guessed, had left with Griff.

'Right. Now we're all here,' Meredith said, 'there's a few things I wanted to say before we start the read-through.' She went through a short list, praising everyone for their work, noting the things that still needed to be done, and commenting how, miraculously, things were running to schedule.

'There's the donors' dinner on Monday, which The Barn restaurant will be catering, and which I hope you're all looking forward to. And we're on track for the first full dress rehearsal on Wednesday,' she said. 'Will the stage be ready for use by then, Jerome?'

Everyone turned to Jerome. Jerome met Meredith's gaze and nodded once.

'Great,' Meredith said. She looked back at her notes and there was a long pause while everyone waited for her to find her place again. Eventually, she raised her head. 'Right. Um. Where were we?'

★ ★ ★

Meredith groaned, pulling the hood of her sweatshirt up to hide her face from Lizzie.

'I don't know,' she said. 'Every time he's near me my tongue gets too big for my mouth and my brain goes on holiday and I can't seem to put a sentence together.'

'But why? Talking is what you do best.'

'That's exactly it,' Meredith said. 'Jerome's different. He's quiet. I can't just chatter away like a goose.'

It was Saturday morning and they'd been sitting in the car outside Hartley House for twenty minutes, finishing the conversation they'd started on the journey from home. There was no scheduled work today, everyone else had the day off, but Lizzie and Meredith were taking the opportunity to sort out some small details and make sure everything was organised and in line. And Lizzie hoped she could go back to the library to do some more reading about Victoria.

With sudden impetus, Meredith pushed her door open and got out. 'Urg!

Enough of this self-torture! It's like being sixteen again.'

The problem was, Lizzie knew, it was impossible to know what Jerome was thinking. And while Meredith would usually be direct enough for the two of them, clearly something was making her shy.

'What about Griff?' Meredith said as they walked across the lawn. It was another warm day; Lizzie slid her sunglasses on against the glare of the white summerhouse.

'What do you mean?'

'You were staring at the restaurant the whole time we were parked,' Meredith teased, bumping her, 'hoping you might see him. Why don't you go over and say hello?'

'I don't want to get in the way,' she said.

She didn't mention Mia, but Meredith guessed that was what she was talking about.

'Poor Oscar,' Meredith said. 'I'm sure he'll be heartbroken when his mum leaves. Even if she does seem a bit of an odd one.' She looped her arm through Lizzie's. 'We'll have to make an extra big fuss of him.'

'But we're not going to be here forever either, are we?' Lizzie said.

Meredith turned to look at her full on. 'My, aren't we a glum pair today?' She clutched Lizzie more tightly again. 'Never mind. We've got to go over and speak to Griff and Claudette about the donors' dinner later, you can find out how things are then.'

'You can handle that without me, can't you?' Lizzie said. 'I wanted to go back to the library for a while.'

'You're not avoiding him, are you?' Meredith said shrewdly.

Before Lizzie could answer, Jerome appeared from the side of the summer-house, carrying his drill. Meredith drew up short. He spied them and raised a hand in greeting. Liz waved back cheerily.

'I didn't know he'd be here,' Meredith whispered from the side of her mouth. 'I haven't even got any make-up on!'

'You're gorgeous without,' Lizzie said. She urged Meredith forward.

'I thought I'd finish up today, since another job has come up for Monday,' Jerome said, approaching them. The sleeves of his soft cotton shirt were rolled high on his tanned forearms.

'Good. Great. Lovely. Thank you,' Meredith said. Lizzie could tell she was trying to hide her disappointment at the news he was finishing.

Jerome smiled, showing a deep cleft of dimple in one cheek, and returned to work. Meredith watched him go, her face falling.

'I definitely talk too much,' she muttered.

9

Lizzie sat on the floor of the library in a slant of sunlight, leafing through a box of letters. They'd been left on the table for her, and she'd soon become absorbed in the work of easing each out of its thick cream envelope and trying to discern who all the characters were in this social network.

The letters were all addressed to Victoria and were dated between 1897 and 1900. Lizzie imagined Victoria had collected them all into this pretty wooden box herself; that it might once have lived in her bedroom or sitting room until, after her death, it was archived here. Lizzie might even be the first person to read these letters since then.

At first, she'd been anxious about entering the library, let alone rifling through Victoria's things, in case Victoria was upset by it. But Waverley was right: the house did feel welcoming, and the letters were a harmless, engrossing glimpse of another life. She barely noticed the hours slipping by.

There were letters from Victoria's mother, instructing her daughter on how to behave while she stayed with her cousin in London. There were letters on pink paper — full of exclamation marks — from one of Victoria's girlfriends, talking with excitement about her upcoming visit and full of breathless enthusiasm for her new puppy. There was a list of 'improving reading' from a pompous young man who referenced having met Victoria at a classical concert (but some of the list was ticked off, so Victoria must have taken it seriously). There were love letters, written with passion and juvenile handwriting, containing lots of quotations from Byron. None of the senders' names on these love letters were repeated more than once. Still, Lizzie made a careful list of every name she came across.

She unfolded a letter addressed 'Dear Cousin,' and signed, 'Your loving cousin, Isabel'.

You have asked me not to mention any of the details in our previous correspondence to your mother, and so I won't — but I daresay she will hear of it somehow, and she might well urge you to caution. As do I. It is not because he is a soldier, dearest. Although it is unfortunate that he hasn't a penny, you must believe me when I tell you this is not my motivation for advising you to resist him.

I have heard about him from Harry's brother. He is well known in many circles. Charming, certainly. Flirtatious with everyone from youngest daughters to widows. Dashing and heroic, I don't have a doubt. His interest in you shows his good taste and I don't believe it is not genuine. But it won't be the first time he has shown such interest to a girl, and while he can move on from it, such attention (and gossip) affects women in different ways.

I know better than to advise you to put some distance between you. All I am asking is: no more midnight picnics.

Please promise to at least consider

what I've said. Do not think that a rogue is romantic and that you can change him. This is real life, my darling, and women's lives have been ruined by such things as this.

The letter was dated August 1899.

Thoughtfully, Lizzie took out the photographs that Waverley had given Meredith, of Victoria and Hartley House that same summer. That was the summer that they had put on the theatre production of their own on the lawn. She looked again at Victoria's freckled face in the group photograph, and then studied more closely the other faces: three more women, and two men posing in their summer suits. One man at the back of the group wasn't looking at the camera like the rest; he was looking at Victoria.

Lizzie turned the photo over and read the names written in faded pencil on the back, counting in to the name that corresponded in the line up to the position of the man.

'Thomas Madden,' she said quietly to

herself.

The name sounded familiar. She flicked back through the stack of letters. Yes, here it was, in one of her girlfriend Esther's pink letters:

I hear Christopher is bringing Lt. Madden with him when he comes down for the summer. Do give him my best regards until I can get there — I'm sure you'll have plenty of fun with them both!

Lieutenant Madden. The image wasn't very clear, but he could definitely be the man Lizzie had seen in the photo on the summerhouse roof. Same fresh face and square jaw. Handsome. The sort of man it might be quite easy to fall for.

And then have your heart broken by.

Poor Victoria. Jilted and humiliated. No wonder there was a bitter streak in her. Lizzie would want to push someone over too.

She just wished Victoria hadn't picked her to vent her frustration on.

'Men,' she muttered, wanting to show solidarity.

The door slammed behind her, making

her jump and scatter the photos. She glanced around, heart racing. The window was closed — there was no draught.

She hurried to the door and reached for the handle, with a terrible sense of dread that something meant to stop her from leaving. But once her hand closed on the handle the door opened easily onto the empty hallway.

Leaving the door fully open, Lizzie returned to the desk to hastily tidy things up and collect her bag.

Enough for today.

★ ★ ★

As she was leaving, she met Oscar coming through the front door.

'Hello!' she said, beaming at him. He stopped inside the threshold and greeted her shyly.

'Not up to anything with Laurel today?' Lizzie asked. 'She's been asking after you.'

Oscar's fair skin coloured slightly. 'My mum's visiting,' he said.

'I know, I met her,' Lizzie said kindly. 'Of course she'd want you all to herself.'

'Yeah. She's not going to be here very long.'

He scratched his ear and looked at the flexing toes of his Converse trainers. But he made no move to leave her, so she ventured, 'My mother wasn't around when I was growing up. Meredith and I were raised by our grandmother. Now it's just the two of us: me and Meredith. Sometimes I dream of having a big family. All the things everyone else had. But then I remember . . . '

'What?'

'No one's got a normal family. There's no such thing.'

Oscar was quiet a moment. Then he said, 'Maybe you will have a really big family one day.'

'Wouldn't that be nice?'

He smiled up at her cheekily. 'Depends who you get.'

She laughed. 'That's very true.'

His smile slowly faded and he looked at his fidgeting feet again as they scuffed the hardwood floor. In a confiding voice, he said, 'I don't know if she — '

'Hi.' Griff arrived in the sun-backed doorway. Lizzie hadn't heard him approach and wondered how long he'd been there. He didn't seem aware that he'd interrupted Oscar, but he might have heard Lizzie talking about family. 'Meredith told me you were working in the library,' he said.

'Yes — I just wanted to. Why? Did you want me?' she said, flustered by his appearance.

'No, I came back to have lunch with Oscar.' He put his hand on Oscar's shoulder and gave him a friendly shake, but Oscar barely responded. Griff looked at him with curiosity.

'Oh — right — of course!' Lizzie started to edge around them to the door, and met Meredith arriving too.

'There you are,' Meredith said. 'I was wondering if you'd finished. Didn't you get my text?' She threaded her arm through Lizzie's and Lizzie gratefully let Meredith take the burden of the conversation.

'Hi there, O. How's my favourite stage hand?'

Oscar smiled up at her as if her attention were a warm ray of sunlight.

'I was wondering if you might be able to help me with something?' Meredith went on. 'I've lost the cigarette case I keep my business cards in — you now, the one you were looking at the other day?'

'Gran's cigarette case?' Lizzie asked, startled.

'You didn't pick it up, did you?' Meredith asked her.

'No,' Lizzie said, 'I haven't seen it.'

'I think it must have fallen out of my bag somewhere. I was hoping O, with his young eyes, might keep a look out for it.' She turned to Oscar hopefully.

Usually Oscar would leap at the chance to do something for Meredith, but he hesitated and glanced uncertainly at Griff. Griff frowned, bemused.

'Of course you'll help, won't you, O?' Griff said.

Lizzie watched Oscar's face with a

sinking sensation. His discomfort went beyond shyness, and she had a suspicion she knew what it was really about.

'Yeah, maybe,' he mumbled.

Lizzie squeezed Meredith's arm covertly. 'We should go. See you on Monday, I hope, Oscar? If your mum can spare you.'

Griff, with a hint of exasperation as he watched Oscar, said shortly, 'Of course she can. She knows Oscar's got his own life.'

Lizzie thought she saw Oscar fold in on himself a little, and she understood how he felt. Griff was clearly just concerned, but it had sounded like a rebuke.

'You two are late for lunch!' Mia called from the top of the staircase, drawing all of their attention. Despite her being so far away, her voice rang clear though the hall. She was bending slightly to see down to them, and her hair waterfalled momentarily to the side; then she straightened up and disappeared without waiting for an answer.

Sound certainly travelled well in this

area of the house, Lizzie thought, making a mental note not to have any private conversations here.

Griff and Oscar shared a glance and said goodbye. Lizzie steered Meredith out of the house.

'I didn't know you'd lost Gran's cigarette case,' she said as they walked. She felt thoroughly discombobulated, and needed some time to pick through everything to find out what was inciting which emotion in her; the ghost, Oscar's secretiveness, or Griff.

'I noticed it missing earlier. It can only be on the grounds somewhere, I haven't been anywhere else since I last had it. I don't know why Oscar didn't want to help — what was that about, do you think?'

'I don't know.' She had no proof of anything, so she didn't like feeling suspicious of Mia. Mia deserved the benefit of the doubt, she reminded herself, determined not to let her feelings about Griff affect her opinion of Mia unfairly.

'Poor Oscar, though,' Meredith

mused. 'He didn't seem very happy, did he?'

* * *

Griff watched Oscar as they headed into the flat. Oscar wouldn't look at him. What was going on? Had his conversation with Lizzie upset him?

Griffin had overheard the last part and regretted having to interrupt, but he didn't want to stand there eavesdropping. Lizzie was so good with Oscar. The little boy worshipped Meredith, but it was Lizzie he seemed instinctively to trust.

Mia was waiting at the door; she scooped Oscar into the crook of her arm and pressed hard, frantic kisses to the crown of his head as if she wanted to eat him up.

'Wash your hands, gorgeous, I've made ham and cheese toasties,' she said. 'You too, gorgeous,' she added to Griff, winking. 'You wouldn't believe the trouble I've had with your grill. It's the most contrary object ever created. The smoke alarm kept going off for no reason.'

Did she notice the quietness in Oscar, or was it impossible amidst her own activity and chatter?

'I thought you said the theatre company wasn't working this weekend,' she said casually as she slid the plates onto the kitchen table.

'They're not,' Griff said. 'Meredith came in to talk to me about a dinner we're catering on Monday.'

Oscar took his seat at the table next to Mia, and she reached to unnecessarily push his hair off his forehead. She'd already told Griff she had preferred Oscar's hair longer.

'And what was she doing in the house?' she said.

'Who, Lizzie?' Griff said. He paused in pouring them all a glass of water from a jug.

'Yes. Lizzie.'

'Waverley said she could use the library to do some research.'

Mia didn't respond. Oscar glanced at

Griff from under his eyelashes, a hint to tread lightly.

Oh. So maybe Mia had seen Oscar talking to Lizzie too. She could be possessive sometimes, when the mood took her. And being cooped up in the flat was obviously putting her into a strange mood. But Griff supposed it was natural to feel insecure when your son was already in someone else's care.

'Are you . . . still going to be around on Monday?' he asked Mia. She'd told him nothing of her plans, and her evasiveness was something else to worry about. She clearly had something on her mind. 'Trying to get rid of me?' she said, taking a bite of toast and grinning at him.

'Of course not. But Meredith invited Oscar to help out at the donors' dinner, and you'd be welcome to come too, if you like.'

She chewed her sandwich slowly. When she looked at Oscar, he sat up straighter.

'Yeah, Mum; come.'

'I'll have to see.' She pinched a cherry

tomato from Oscar's plate and popped it into her mouth. 'You know I don't like planning too far ahead.'

Griff bit back a reply. He rubbed his temples wearily instead. They would need to have a proper conversation soon.

'Are you all right?' Oscar asked him.

Griff smiled at him. Oscar noticed everything.

'I'm fine. Just a bit of a headache.'

'You're taking on too much,' Mia said.

He laughed shortly. That much was true.

After lunch, while Oscar cleared the table, Griff looked around the flat, wondering if he could spare some time to clean it up. There were piles of folded laundry on the furniture, dirty mugs, half the contents of the food cupboards out on the counter. He could almost see his mother standing by the sink with her arms folded, shaking her head in dismay. The chaos made him feel inwardly chaotic too. But he needed to get back to the restaurant, and he'd also promised to help Waverley go through the job applications he'd received for the new groundsman's job.

Outside the window, the pear tree shivered its branches in the breeze and lost the last of the leaves it had spent all morning shedding. The tree's thick, gnarly branches were as sturdy as ever, but to look at it you would think it was winter.

10

Lizzie had stolen a book from the library, but only by accident. When Meredith wasn't travelling, the two of them had a Sunday ritual: a yoga class, followed by an indulgent brunch, followed by Lizzie doing the ironing while Meredith vacuumed the house. But that afternoon it was much too warm for housework, so Lizzie put up no resistance to Meredith's suggestion that they go out instead.

They ended up at a small village pub and spent the afternoon in the beer garden. While Meredith half-dozed over her scripts for the next recordings of Bedtime Stories, Lizzie fought a wasp for her lemonade and dug in her bag for something of her own to read.

She must have picked up the slender paperback with all her other stuff in her haste to leave the library yesterday, although she didn't remember seeing it on the desk.

As I Remember It, by Esther King.

Lizzie flipped the book over to the photograph of the author on the back cover. In it, Esther was in her late seventies, with smooth, backcombed blond hair, pearls around her neck over a black polo neck, and a cigarette in her relaxed hand. The photo, and the style of the book, were quite dated, and Lizzie read on the flyleaf that it had been published in 1960.

'Esther King,' Lizzie mused. 'Why is that name familiar?'

She flipped back through her notes from yesterday. Of course: Esther of the pink notepaper and exclamation marks. Apparently she had gone on to become a renowned dog breeder, and in her seventies she'd written her autobiography.

Lizzie turned the pages, not especially absorbed by the many details or photographs of the dogs Esther had kept in her life (Lizzie was more of a cat person), but she did find Esther's burgeoning feminism interesting.

Esther had been greatly shaped, she

wrote, by the death of one of her closest friends. Though Esther never named
her, she described a young mother who
had never recovered her health after suf-
fering a broken heart in her youth.

'She was treated unbearably cruelly
by a monstrous man,' Esther wrote, 'who
strung her along and showed the most
sincere sort of interest, and then one
day, eyeing a better proposition, simply
disappeared from her life. Of course,
she was blamed for her part in his bad
behaviour, when all she had done was let
herself be seduced. He, however, went
on to prove his character by deserting
from the army. She was hurt twice: by
him, and then by a society that refused
to forgive her and stunted her prospects.'

Esther had joined the suffragettes,
and in the first world war volunteered
with the Red Cross. The upending of the
world had been the making of her.

Meredith broke off from her reading
with a yawn.

'Hey,' she said, her chin on her folded
hands, 'do you think we should head off

and find something to eat?'

Lizzie put down her book and stretched her shoulders. The afternoon was cooling and she could smell the jasmine planted in the beds behind them. Instead of answering, she grinned at Meredith.

'What?' Meredith said.

'Big day tomorrow, with the donors' dinner. Big week coming up. This time next week you'll be on stage . . . '

'Is that smile a touch of hysteria?'

'A bit,' Lizzie said. 'I suddenly felt a touch of Sunday night panic. Which is weird, because I've loved every part of the last few days.' Except being shoved by a ghost and scared out of my wits, she thought. But even then . . . there was something exhilarating about Hartley House.

'Can you be excited and terrified at the same time?' she said.

'You've just described every opening night of my life,' Meredith laughed then she said, 'Have I told you I'm proud of you?'

Lizzie felt a warmth spread through her chest and almost blushed at the unexpectedness of it. 'Never in my life,' she said.

'Oh.' Meredith stood up, shouldering her bag. 'Well, maybe one day I will.'

Lizzie swatted her with Esther's book.

'You know, you should ask Fatima for some help with your research,' Meredith said as left the pub. 'She's really into those family history websites, if you're looking for records.'

'That might be a good idea,' Lizzie said thoughtfully.

'What are you hoping to find out, anyway?'

'What reason Victoria might have for haunting the house.'

Meredith gave her the side-eye.

'You and your ghosts,' she muttered.

11

On Monday, after another day of rehears-
als, Lizzie got dressed for the donors'
dinner in the summerhouse with the
other girls. In between putting on her
third coat of mascara and complaining
about the itchiness of wigs, Fatima told
Lizzie the result of the research Lizzie
had asked her to do.

'I found a Thomas Madden born on
4th May 1870, but haven't got a death
date for him yet,' she said.

'Is that unusual?'

'Not very,' Fatima said. 'Not all the
records are kept in the same place. There
are a few other websites I could try. It
was up to the next of kin to register a
death — maybe he didn't have any. Or
maybe he died abroad, or at sea. There
could be lots of reasons.'

'What about a marriage record?'

'None that I found.'

Lizzie thanked her, and helped her

tie her bowtie. When that was done, she extended a hand and tilted Fatima's ridiculously tall hat to a jaunty angle. Fatima had to wobble her head to keep it on. They fell into giggles.

The Mad Hatter costume was one of Lizzie's favourites.

In keeping with the Alice in Wonderland theme, Lizzie wore a late Victorian-style dress made of pale green muslin, with an emerald sash belt. It had such a low hem that she was anxious about tripping over it, given how accident prone she was these days. But Meredith insisted. A dozen generous patrons were attending the al fresco Mad Hatter's tea party, and since there would be entertainment from the actors (a preview of their performances) they would all be in costume.

Meredith, dressed as the Queen of Hearts, looked — unsurprisingly — stunning. Kate had made the dress especially for her. The scarlet fabric of the structured corset with its black laces, and the ruby full skirts, with matching lipstick, made her look bold and imperious.

While the others were putting the finishing touches to their outfits, Lizzie took the first opportunity she'd had that day to return the book she'd unwittingly pinched to the library.

'Give me five minutes,' she told Meredith. 'I'll be back before our guests start arriving.'

She crossed to the main house with the book in her hand. It was a strange experience to sashay about in the long, full skirt; such a thing definitely made a girl walk differently. She imagined herself as one of those women in pictures of deportment lessons, with a pile of books on her head, and straightened her spine.

'Goodness!' a voice said as she stepped through the door. 'I thought I was seeing one of my ancestors for a moment then.'

Waverley came towards her from the small room that was his office, and she noticed he was hobbling slightly, though he had his customary smile.

'Don't you look a picture,' he said.

Lizzie flushed and resisted giving him a twirl. 'Thank you. Wait till you see

Meredith, she's gorgeous.' She held the book to her chest. 'Are you all right?' She made a subtle gesture to his leg.

'It's nothing really, just a touch of sciatica. Blasted nuisance, makes it hard to get around.

I'll still be coming to the dinner tonight, but you may have to excuse me early.'

'I'm sorry to hear that. Is there anything I can do for you?'

'How kind. Thank you, but Griff's been keeping a close eye on me, bringing me ice packs and painkillers. Couldn't manage without him.'

He pointing enquiringly at the book.

'Oh!' Lizzie said, embarrassed. 'I picked this up by mistake the other day — I was about to return it to the library. I'm so sorry, I didn't mean to walk out with it . . . '

'No harm done,' he said. 'I imagine it was helpful to you in some way?'

'Yes, actually. Especially the part about your grandmother.'

'There's a part about my grandmother;

is that so?' he said, intrigued.

'I assumed that was why you left it out for me?'

'No, I wasn't aware. Perhaps I'll take a look at it.'

Lizzie offered it to him but he held up a hand. 'Oh no, I think you should return it to the library. There might be something else in there for you.'

'Um . . . okay.' She frowned and then laughed. 'I'll just put it on the desk.'

'Thank you, Lizzie.'

She nodded and turned towards the library, aware that Waverley was still there, watching her go. In the early evening light, the library glowed orange, and with the rows and rows of brown-trunked books lining the walls it was almost like stepping into a forest. She slid Esther's book onto the polished table with a sound like a whisper. After the bustle of the preparations for the evening, the solitude was a soothing break.

When she thought over what Waverley had said it seemed obvious that he meant he'd left something else for her to read, so she scanned the desk for what it might be. There was nothing new in the neat piles of scrapbooks beside Victoria's wooden box of letters. But on the shelf beside the desk she noticed a gap, which was probably the spot where Esther's book lived. She picked up the book again and made to slot it into place, but felt a slight resistance, and heard a crumpling sound.

Lizzie took the book back and reached into the gap to retrieve a creased square of notepaper. She unfolded it.

Dear Isabel, she read. *Thank you for your warnings, which I know you only give because you care for me. But you are wrong about Thomas. While he will barely catch my eye in company, I am the one who flirts and takes his arm. I am the one who ensures my seat is always next to his and steals place settings to make it so. I am the one who entreats him to come and find me. Don't be cross with Thomas, he is an angel. I adore him. I can't help it. And we mean to be together, to make our life together, no matter what my father thinks of him, or what he may do, because I know I can never be apart from Thomas now. He has promised me.*

The letter ended in the middle of the page. Unsigned. Unsent.

Lizzie drew it closer to her face and breathed in the scent of the paper. She expected the musty, woody smell of the bookshelves, but it smelled sweetly of lavender and carnations.

She refolded the paper and slipped it into the back of the wooden box, with Victoria's other letters.

12

The first guests were arriving. On the lawn near the summerhouse a long table had been set up, with a white tablecloth, and an array of picnic food so gloriously enticing it had everyone's mouth watering and their fingers itching. The siren call of Claudette's food was something you never got used to.

In the centre of the table was a sugar fondant dormouse asleep beside a teapot made of red velvet sponge cake.

A waitress dressed in formal black and white, and with black and white striped tights to match, was opening a bottle of wine. Laurel, who had on a pair of white rabbit's ears on a headband, and a teeshirt designed with a giant pocket watch, waited eagerly for her cue to show the patrons to their seats, as soon as Meredith had greeted them.

Oscar, who was to be Laurel's partner in her ushering duties that night, hadn't arrived yet. Lizzie hoped he hadn't decided not to come.

'You're late!' Meredith murmured to her when Lizzie joined her. Meredith had already seen their first guests seated.

'Sorry. How's it going?'

'So far so good. Good weather, food looks amazing . . . 'She trailed off, gazing past Lizzie's shoulder.

More guests had arrived: Jacintha and Jocasta Buckley, two elderly sisters who were well known for supporting the theatre, the ballet, galleries and all kinds of arts. They generously funded them with part of the large income they had made from having invented a microchip for a dishwasher some decades ago.

And behind them: Jerome. In a tuxedo.

Lizzie watched Meredith's whole being catch alight.

'I invited him,' she whispered to Meredith.

Meredith turned to her, flustered and speechless.

'It was either that,' Lizzie said, 'or

never see him again.' She gave Meredith a gentle shove. 'Go and say hello. I'll take care of the Buckley sisters.'

Meredith nodded politely to the ladies as she slid past them to greet Jerome. Lizzie came forward and shook their hands warmly. 'It's so nice to see you both again.'

'I suppose we can't expect to compete,' Jocasta said with a twinkle, smiling as they all watched Meredith approach her dashing companion. Jerome looked surprisingly comfortable in a tux. Lizzie thought she heard a wistful sigh from Jacintha.

'You both could compete for anything in those wonderful outfits,' Lizzie said.

They wore their signature purple: Jocasta in a floor-length sleeveless dress with a white cashmere wrap; Jacintha in a pale pink trouser suit with a purple scarf knotted around her long white hair. Lizzie hoped she had half their style at their age. Actually, she'd settle for half their style now.

'Are you going to be performing this

evening?' Jacintha asked her.

'No,' Lizzie laughed. 'I'll be leaving that to our talented actors. I'm afraid Meredith got all those genes in our family.'

She left them to Laurel to guide them to their seats, and turned to greet some more newcomers. Meredith was still standing with Jerome, the two of them talking in low voices, tentatively smiling at one another.

As the table began to fill and the music of murmuring voices and laughter sounded through the garden, Lizzie saw two more figures coming to join them from the house: Waverley, with a slightly stiff walk, and Oscar, who helped him to a chair near the Buckley sisters.

And then, with his white rabbit ears bobbing on their headband, Oscar dashed to Laurel. The two shared a gleeful hug. Lizzie was delighted he'd made it.

She saw Griff too: off to the side, giving directions to one of the waiting staff. He was too busy to notice her, but she drank in the sight of him in his dark suit:

his calm, unobtrusive manner, keeping everything running smoothly.

Daniel — the Cheshire Cat in pink and purple stripes — bounced onto the grass, did a cartwheel and a somersault, touched the gas lighter in his hand to the unlit brazier on the side of the stage and lit up the flame. The audience 'oohed' and then all fell silent in anticipation.

Oscar and Laurel dropped to sit cross-legged on the grass in front of the stage. The waiting staff watched for glasses that needed refilling and awaited their cue to uncover the silver-domed platters in the centre of the table that hid the sweetest of treats.

But first there was the Cheshire Cat, and his daring acrobatics on the climbing frame of a tree that Jerome had built, as he recited a welcome to Wonderland.

Lizzie, standing at the back of the crowd, felt every inch of her flesh tingle. The firelight, the smell of wine, the sense of being transported to another world . . . To her, the theatre was magic.

Following Daniel, Kate gave a taste of her performance as Alice, with a very funny recital of the poem 'You are Old, Father William'. The entertainment then paused to give everyone a chance to eat dinner. The guests chatted freely over Claudette's Drink Me soup (cucumber and watercress) and Eat Me loaves (Rosemary and Pecorino). They ate crumpets and fondant fancies and scones with jam and cream. Lizzie spied Oscar pinch a third jam tart.

She was kept busy talking to patrons, taking photographs, and answering a costume crisis when the stitching holding together Fatima's top hat fell apart (Fatima would be following dinner with a magic show, and the hat was where she kept her coloured handkerchiefs).

Throughout the evening Lizzie was always aware of Griff. He was organising the waiting staff, he was encouraging Oscar not to get too over-excited, he was bringing blankets to anyone who needed warmth, or bringing Waverly his cane and chiding him about sitting for too long, all in between nipping back to the restaurant to fulfil his duties there too. He was calm, competent, and at ease.

And once, when he crossed behind her, she felt a feather touch at the small of her back, and the nearness of him as he bent to answer the diner beside her made her catch her breath. But they didn't speak.

Fatima's magic show was a hit; then it was Meredith's turn.

By that time most of the guests were pleasantly tipsy. The evening was nearly over; there was only a thin banner of twi-lit sky at the horizon and the rest was dark. Fatima had left them gasping and laughing. Meredith came to the centre of the stage with her guitar in one hand and a stool in the other. She set down the stool, perched on it, and balanced the guitar against her body as she reached to let down the pins in her hair and shake the blond waves loose.

No sound but the leaves and the flut-tering tablecloth.

Meredith put her fingertips to the strings and bent her head to the instrument. She played a few notes, and began to sing.

It was the perfect end-of-night song, melancholy but not downbeat, full of nostalgia and bittersweet emotion. Meredith's husky-pure voice and her unshowy delivery had them all spellbound.

Lizzie snapped a photo of her sister, and then lowered the camera and just watched. She was again at the back of the group, standing removed from the candlelit party, and she could see across the rapt faces of the audience. She could see Jerome sitting at the end of the long table, his lips slightly parted, and saw him falling for Meredith. Everyone did, when she sang. Or maybe he had fallen for her long ago and was only now stripped of his reserve and showing it.

Lizzie felt a thrill of joy. How wonderful for Meredith to inspire feelings like that, to have someone look at her like that.

It had always been this way. Lizzie

facilitated, kept records, carried the sewing kit . . . Meredith was the star. Lizzie was full of pride and admiration for her sister. But still. Still . . .

To know, just once, what that felt like.

She had to look away, biting her lip. Being daft. The music getting to her.

Glancing up again, her eyes met Griff's. He was also behind the crowd, a little distance behind Jerome, and while everyone else was watching Meredith, he was looking at her.

She caught her breath. He held her gaze steadily, and half smiled. She blushed at the unexpected attention.

'What?' she mouthed, giddily.

He gave a gentle shrug. 'You look amazing,' he mouthed back, and she felt light-headed.

His gaze didn't leave hers until Meredith's song ended and everyone applauded.

Meredith's second song was more upbeat, to leave the audience on a high. Laurel jumped up and she and Oscar began to dance on the grass. Griff's attention was stolen by the waiter. Lizzie took a long breath and tried to gather herself.

'Your sister is very talented,' said Mia, sidling up to Lizzie, startling her. Lizzie hadn't seen her approach from the house.

'Thanks. I think so too,' she said in a friendly tone, trying not to show how distracted she was by Griff. 'You should have come down earlier and had something to eat.'

Mia stopped close to Lizzie. She was barefoot, curling her toes in the grass. There was something familiar and almost possessive about the gesture, as if she were walking the carpets of her own home.

'It must be hard, surrounded by all these extroverts,' Mia said, 'when you're more of the backstage type.'

Lizzie caught herself self-consciously pulling on the sash at her waist.

'Sometimes,' she agreed. 'But I like to think we compliment each other.'

Mia was dressed in cropped jeans

and a t-shirt, and Lizzie wondered if she ought to turn her away for not fitting in with the dress code. But perhaps it wouldn't be necessary; Mia seemed to have no intention of joining the party, only looking. Maybe she was just checking on Oscar.

'Oscar's done a great job tonight,' Lizzie added.

'Did you get some photos of him?' Mia asked. 'I'd love to see them.'

'Sure.'

Lizzie scrolled back through the pictures until she found some shots of Oscar and Laurel. She passed the camera to Mia, and Mia looked at them with a wistful expression.

'You can see how big he's getting,' she murmured.

'Must be all the fresh air.'

'And all the biscuits Griff is feeding him.' She smiled at Lizzie. 'I'm glad they've got such a good relationship. I'm glad Oscar is growing up here. It's such a special place. For all three of us.' She returned the camera to Lizzie. 'I really like the idea of the bond me and Griff have from all our history here continuing on through Oscar.'

Lizzie couldn't think of anything to say. She fiddled with the camera, scrolling back through images of the dinner and the performances — even a picture of Griff she'd managed to take while he was bending to chat to Jocasta Buckley. She wondered if he'd noticed that Mia was here. Probably; he was aware of everything.

'It's like Oscar is continuing a family tradition,' Mia went on.

And I'm just a visitor, Lizzie thought. I can't compete with that.

Meredith started an encore, and Fatima and Daniel went among the guests to choose dance partners and urge them to their feet. Waverley, despite his sciatica, invited Jacintha to join him in a wobbly waltz, bowing chivalrously over her hand.

Lizzie scanned the figures for Griff, and eventually caught sight of him heading back to the restaurant, fading into shadow as he went.

'It would be easy to feel eclipsed,' Mia said.

Lizzie glanced at her in question, and Mia nodded towards Meredith.

'By such a glittering sister, I mean,' Mia said. 'I certainly would.'

Lizzie again stared after Griff, feeling oddly deflated. She thought of Victoria's letter, her full-hearted devotion to Thomas, who turned out not to be deserving, not to be suitable, not to be a good guy. Stringing her along with false impressions and promises he couldn't keep.

13

Griff closed up the restaurant, knowing everyone would be leaving the donors' dinner about now. The waiting staff had returned the crockery and cutlery to the kitchen and the sugar fondant animals had been parcelled up for the guests to take home as a souvenir. When he locked the restaurant doors, he saw Claudette and Laurel driving off, leaving the car park almost empty.

He stood outside the doors a moment, rolling his shoulders. Maybe he should stay an extra hour and check the rosters for next week. First, he should check the grounds of the summerhouse; the table could be left until morning, but he should make sure there was no mess or litter. But before that he should look in on Oscar and Mia. There was still that conversation to be had with Mia. And he needed to make sure Waverley was ok and didn't need any help getting settled for the evening.

There were emails that needed answering, accounts that needed updating, an application to write for Oscar's after-school clubs next term.

It was the end of an overwhelming day, and he felt clobbered by a sense that no matter how fast he was running, he was still falling behind.

He passed a hand over his eyes wearily, not knowing where to start. At the sound of a footstep in the gravel driveway he was slow to look up. But when he did, seeing Lizzie there was like having the fog clear from his head, leaving only what was essential.

I should have asked her to dance, he thought with sudden clarity, instead of running off when I saw her with Mia.

She still wore the green muslin dress, but he was amused to see that she had trainers on her feet, which made her more Lizzie than Victorian lady. She paused a few feet away.

'Hey.' She clasped her hands in front of her. 'I know you probably don't need it — I'm sure you've got everything under control — I just thought I would hang around a while, in case maybe . . . possibly . . . you might need some help?'

He took a deep breath and felt his chest ease where he hadn't even known it was tight. The tension in his shoulders unknotted.

'I'm glad you're here,' he said.

She broke into a radiant smile. 'You are?'

Heavens, she was transparent. It made her feel protective of her, but at the same time it made him want to be as open as she was, and right then he was too weary to keep his defences up anyway.

'It's been a tough day,' he said, 'and I really wanted to see you.'

She took a step forward, angling her heart towards him like an offering.

'You've got me,' she said.

14

He fretted as he weighed a bundle of keys in his hand.

'I need to check on Oscar.'

'He went home with Mia, practically dead on his feet.'

'Waverley hasn't been well . . . '

'I think the dancing did him good. I walked him back to the house and he was practically skipping.' 'I've got to read through some job applications for Waverley.'

'Tonight? Why?'

'I said I would.'

She gave him a long look. The tiredness was written all over him. She wanted to reach out and run her palm over his cheek, like her grandmother always did to her when she was fatigued by the world.

'Well,' she said, 'can I help you out with that?'

He cocked his head, half smiled in wonder.

'Now, that would be a wasted opportunity, wouldn't it?'

As if on impulse, he reached out his hand to her, and she took it without hesitation.

'Let's go for a walk,' he said, already moving, pulling her after him.

She had made her decision. Like Victoria, she wouldn't resist her feelings but give in wholeheartedly to them. Victoria couldn't know she was pinning her hopes on the wrong man. Neither could Lizzie know if she was; whether Mia would always own the bulk of Griff's heart, or whether any of a million things would come between them. But Griff was worth the risk. She trusted him.

★ ★ ★

It was nearly midnight. Griff used the torch app on his phone to light the way as they headed down to the cove. The narrow shoreline was a mixture of shingle and sand, with hump-backed rocks rising in the dark, full of shallow pool life. The sea went on with its timeless business, swishing gentle waves.

'That's the way the smugglers go,' Griff teased, pointing to an opening in the base of the cliff that led into cavernous dark. 'Did Waverley tell you about that?'

Lizzie nodded, gazing with interest. Perhaps in the daylight it wasn't so sinister, but in the dark you couldn't tell what was rubble and what was shadow; it looked unsafe and not a little creepy. On the side closest to them she saw a drift of litter caught in sparse dry reeds: a cigarette packet, a sandwich bag. An ugly bit of an otherwise pretty place.

'Where does it lead?' she said.

'It comes out behind the folly, and then on into town. They dug it out, hundreds of years ago, to make it easier to hide contraband in there.'

He took her hand again to help her over a line of bladderwrack left by the outgoing tide. She still managed to bring her foot down on it, sliding on the slippery seaweed, and caught him tighter to right herself.

'This is going to be our 'thing', isn't it?' he said, waving a hand between them, referencing the number of times he'd caught her when she was off balance. She flushed, but smiled. At least they had an in joke. A small rowboat was beached on the sand behind one of the rocks, and Griff led her towards it.

'Not exactly seaworthy condition,' he said, 'but pretty fair for stargazing.'

She stepped into the boat. Its weather-beaten boards creaked under her weight. With its faded paintwork and worm-eaten seats, it looked like it had been here almost as long as the beach had, but the warm weather had left it dry, if a little dirty.

'Your suit!' she said in warning, as he stepped in after her.

'Your dress,' he noted in return. They were neither of them dressed for clamouring about a shipwreck.

She certainly didn't want to give up this opportunity, though, so she shrugged, gathered her skirts around her, and sat down.

Griff took off his jacket. He folded it into a long pillow and set it against the edge of the seat, and Lizzie lay flat with her head on the cushion he had made for her.

She didn't know what was more overwhelming: the spilled glitter pot of stars above her, or Griff's dark head against her shoulder as they shared the view of the sky.

They were quite for a long time. Lizzie listened to the soothing rhythm of the sea and licked the taste of salt air off her lips.

'What will you do next?' Griff asked her, eventually breaking the silence.

'What do you mean?'

'After the play finishes. Where will you go?'

It made her stomach hurt to think of this ending.

'Back to my usual job, probably,' she said.

He turned his ear towards her, but she was still behind him and they couldn't see each other's face. 'Which is?'

'Admin for a pet supply store.'

Griff was quiet again. Lizzie wondered if he was offended by its un-glamorousness. Then he said, 'That is not what I would have guessed for you.'

She fiddled with the sash on her dress again. 'No? What would you have guessed?'

'Researcher. Writer. Theatre producer extraordinaire.'

She ducked her head, smiling. She wasn't going to mention the second written script on her desk at home, the one based on an original story from her own imagination. 'I don't think they give out job titles with 'extraordinaire' in them. My employers were really good in letting me have a month off to do this, but it was always going to be temporary.' She paused. 'Still, there's always the hope we may get funding to tour the show. You know, depending on how well it does . . . '

He sat up and swivelled around to look at her properly, though it wasn't easy to see in the moonlight.

'Oh, well, there you go. It's a given.'

She laughed. 'You think so?'

'I think it's clear you're all very talented. Why shouldn't it be a success?'

'I don't know if it's ever going to be the same in a place that's not here,' Lizzie said softly. 'There's something about this house . . .'

Griff moved away from her, to sit propped against the side of the boat, his feet flat and his wrists hanging over his knees. After another long pause, he said, 'What are you researching in the library?'

'I've been reading about Waverley's grandmother, Victoria.'

'Why?'

She sat up too. His white shirt glowed an ethereal blue, but his face was mostly in shadow.

'Are you cold?' she asked.

'I'm fine.'

She straightened up, putting her feet together and looking at her trainers as they rested in the bottom of the boat.

'She was in love with a soldier before she married Waverley's grandfather,' she said. 'His name was Thomas Madden,

147

and they did a play outside the summer-house, a hundred and twenty years ago. It fascinates me.' She glanced at him, trying to make out his features in the low light. 'It's like you said, the past feels like it's hardly separated from us at all.'

He looked at her thoughtfully. She found herself shivering, hugging her arms around herself. It always felt precarious, discussing Victoria, as though she was inviting disaster. She remembered again the sharp kick at the back of her knee. But they were far from the house here.

'What happened to him?' Griff asked. 'The soldier?'

'He was a bit of a cad. Broke her heart, disappeared one day. Deserted from the army. I've been wondering, actually, whether Victoria's father may have paid him off. Maybe it was always about the money . . .'

She shrugged. The theory had occurred to her some time after she'd spoken to Fatima about Thomas, but as she said it aloud, she didn't like the sound of it.

It made sense, and it was the kind of thing that happened; Victoria's father clearly had a flexible sense of morality... but it felt sordid, sour in her mouth.

She rubbed her arms, still feeling a chill. To turn the conversation, she sat forward and said, 'Are you sure you're not cold?'

Griff didn't have a chance to answer.

The little boat tipped suddenly; Lizzie felt the ground shift beneath them as if a shelf of sand had fallen away. She was thrown sideways. She put out a hand to catch herself, but heard a loud thunk as Griff's head struck wood.

For a long moment of apprehension she balanced, arms outstretched, but the boat had seemingly settled firm.

'Ow . . . ' Griff moaned.

'Are you ok?' She scooted towards him.

He untangled one arm from where it had become wedged under the seat, and held his other hand to his brow.

'Let me see,' she insisted. Heart

thumping, she took out her phone to see by the light of its screen, and held it up to his face.

'It's ok, it's nothing. Are you all right?' he said.

'Let me see,' she insisted.

Amused by her bossiness, he dropped his hand and let her examine his brow and temple. There was a mark, a darkening splotch, spreading across his forehead.

'Looks like you might have a bruise,' she said. She held up three fingers. 'How many fingers?'

'Three.'

'Does it hurt? Do you feel ok?'

'It's nothing, Lizzie, really.'

'Stay there.'

She jumped out of the boat and walked down to the gently hushing waves. The water was cold, though not unbearably so, when she dipped her untied sash into it.

She returned to Griff. 'Here.'

Kneeling beside him again, she moved to press the folded sash against the bump rising on his forehead.

'Lizzie, really,' he said, resisting, catching her wrist.

'Griff. Let someone take care of you for once.'

His body stiffened, but then softened, and he allowed her to place the compress. After a moment he said, 'Actually, that does feel nice.'

He still had hold of her wrist and under the excuse of playing nurse, she brushed the hair back from his forehead.

'What happened?' he asked.

She hesitated. 'I don't know. But maybe we should leave.'

Griff lifted his right arm and turned it, inspecting, and wincing as he did so. It was the arm that had been wedged under the seat. When Lizzie looked under the seat, she saw a jagged poke of wooden rib there. Griff's sleeve was darkening and sticking to his arm.

'It's just a scratch,' he said.

The smell of his blood mixed with the salt air.

Lizzie gripped the seat with both

hands but it wasn't enough; she was swept away.

Her vision narrowed. Her hearing closed off. She could only hear her own blood rushing and her breath shallow and fast. She turned away from Griff, slumping, and gulped at the air.

Where before they had been alone, now there was another figure on the beach. A woman in a white dress, walking across the shore towards the mouth of the smugglers' tunnel.

Lizzie felt a foreboding. She wanted to call out to the woman not to go inside. It wasn't unlike a nightmare when, almost awake but still paralysed with sleep, you couldn't shout or run or fight back against the monsters. Lizzie's jaw was glued shut. Closer and closer the figure went to the tunnel. Lizzie didn't know why she so dreaded the woman going inside, only that the emotion was so strong in her that she felt almost as if she herself were the one in danger.

At the last moment the woman stopped. She raised her arm and pointed a finger into the dark tunnel. And then she turned and looked directly at Lizzie.

Lizzie gasped and jerked upright, as if waking. Griff was beside her, tenderly holding her face in his hands, turning it to give her the intense and anchoring contact of his gaze. His eyes glittered in the moonlight.

'Are you all right?' he said. 'Are you with me?'

'You're the one who's hurt,' she said, ashamed and perturbed, every muscle weak.

'Maybe we should share the cold compress,' he said lightly, but she could see the concern in him.

With determination she sat up and before he could react, took gentle hold of his wounded arm. He was right: it was just a graze, and not deep. The bleeding had stopped already.

She wound the sash around the injury and the torn sleeve, joking, 'Who would imagine a sash belt could be so multi-functional? Do you think that's why they wore them?'

He gave himself over to her, letting her complete the task, but watching her protectively. As she focussed on what she was doing the fog in her head cleared and she began to feel more grounded.

'Thank you,' he said.

'I'm generally all right after the initial shock. I'm sorry about that.'

'Like I said before, it's a medical condition. You've got nothing to apologise for.'

'It doesn't usually come up so much in day to day life.'

'There do seem to be an unlikely number of accidents around you,' Griff observed.

Lizzie swallowed. 'Maybe I'm being haunted.'

She smiled, a little too late.

Griff didn't smile back. He seemed about to say something, but stopped himself. 'Let's get out of here,' he said instead.

14

They went back to the restaurant, so not to disturb Mia and Oscar. In the kitchen, amid the shining metal surfaces and shelves, Griff found a First Aid Kit, and Lizzie felt a sense of déjà vu.

'Let me do it,' she offered, taking the gauze and bandages from him.

'Are you sure?'

'I'm sure. As long as there's some left-over red velvet cake for afterwards.'

She was a little queasy and needed something to boost her blood sugar. Still, nothing in her life made her as proud as managing to take care of Griff, cleaning the graze on his arm and taping down the gauze. She checked his head too, brushing back his hair to see the purpling bruise, pretending her heart didn't hammer as she did it. He gazed up at her, his head low.

'So,' he said seriously. 'This haunting.'

She set about finding the cake, forks

and plates, so she wouldn't have to see his face as she spoke. But she didn't waver as she said, 'It's Victoria. I saw her the first time when I fell off the ladder, when I was faint. Then, the afternoon of Oscar's party, when I tripped in the stables, that was her. I felt her push me. And today . . . tipping the boat . . . I saw her afterwards. I saw her outside the smugglers' tunnel.'

She was afraid to look at him, afraid to see disbelief, or unease.

'I believe you,' he said.

'You do?' Now she stared hard at him, to see if he was joking. 'You don't think I'm crazy?'

'You're entirely bonkers. But I'll tell you a secret: all the best people are.'

She saw the teasing line of his lip and grinned suddenly. He was quoting *Alice's Adventures in Wonderland*.

'I know this house has ghosts,' he said.

His expression became more pensive. Lizzie thought she understood. He'd lived here with his mother. In any place you lived with someone you loved, there were ghosts, but hopefully they were friendly ones.

He turned the plate of cake, pushing it across the counter to her.

'Here. Eat. You're awfully pale.'

She found she had an appetite for it now, and dug into the implausibly-coloured cake, taking a chunk thick with icing onto her fork. Griff dug his own fork in from the other side, but let it rest on the edge of the plate without tasting it.

'When I lived here as a teenager,' Griff said, 'we lived in the same apartment I live in now. My mum was pretty strict; she had high expectations for me, and she wanted me to do well. I, however, just wanted to see my girlfriend. So I used to climb out of my window and down the pear tree outside . . .'

'It's a lovely tree,' Lizzie said, bemused as to where the story was going. 'A perfect climbing tree.'

'You've seen it?'

She nodded, licking icing off her fork. The sweetness was moreish and intoxicating.

'That tree was struck by lightning in the 1940s and was cut down,' Griff said. 'That tree's not really there.'

Lizzie lowered her fork, frowning.

'It's true,' he said. 'Take a look tomorrow. It may have fruit, or it may have buds. It may not be there at all. It's been gone for a long time, but it seems to be back now, and it's there most days. I think it likes being around us.'

'Being around you . . . ' Lizzie echoed.

'It's friendly. You can feel it.' He wagged his fork at her. 'Now you think I'm crazy.'

'No, I . . . ' She thought back to when she'd stood under the tree, and had actually talked to it. 'I think I know what you mean.'

'Oscar's quite fond of it. Waverley expresses no surprise at all. Mia even ate a pear from it once. It put her to sleep — like a character in a fairy-tale.'

'But it's so substantial,' Lizzie said. 'It's real.'

'Yup.' He watched her face, as if to

remind her that she was the one who had started this mad conversation. 'I think it's become stronger the more notice we take of it. We expect it to be there now, and so it is.'

Lizzie flattened some cake under the prongs of the fork. The crumbs rose up in the spaces between, making neat rows.

'Do you think that's true of Victoria too?' she said.

'It could be. It could be that you were the first person able to see her and now she's trying to get your attention.'

'She doesn't have to try so hard,' Lizzie muttered. 'I don't know why she wants to hurt me.'

'The two times you saw her, you were about to faint. Maybe she doesn't wish you harm, she's just trying to communicate.'

He tentatively touched his forehead, fingering the bruise.

'Although, to keep yourself safe, maybe you should spend less time here,' he added.

Her heart sank. 'I don't want to do that.'

'I don't want you to either, but I don't want you to be hurt.'

'I'd rather stay. Carry on with the research. Maybe I can find out what she wants that way.' She brushed cake crumbs off the counter. 'But I understand if you want me to keep my distance. I'm sorry you got caught up in this.'

'It's my home,' Griff said. 'That's why I'm caught up in this. And please don't keep your distance. I kind of like having you around.'

She smiled again. Despite the drama of the evening, her usual optimism was rising up again. How amazing it was, she thought, to have found this place, to be listening to what Griff was telling her. Ghosts. The supernatural. All the astonishing things that she had always believed existed in the universe, just hidden from sight.

Maybe she could find a different way to communicate with Victoria, she thought. Something less life-threatening.

'Mia wasn't rude to you earlier, was she?' Griff asked suddenly.

'No,' Lizzie said hesitantly, wondering how she could describe what Mia had been.

'She's feeling a little insecure about all the time Oscar is spending with the theatre company. She can get defensive sometimes.'

Lizzie didn't answer. Then she said again,' It's ok. She wasn't rude.'

'I think she'll be leaving soon. I'm not quite sure what her plans are.'

'Oscar will miss her.'

'Unless she packs him up and takes him with her!' Griff chuckled, but his laughter sounded forced.

Gently, Lizzie said, 'Are you worried that might happen?'

'No!' He got up, cleared the plates. 'I doubt it. I mean, that's not the arrangement . . . She was the one who . . . ' He turned his back to her, running water into the sink over the dirty dishes. 'No. It's just me, worrying.'

Lizzie got up and came to stand behind him. She put a soft hand on his back, feeling his shoulder blade beneath the smooth cotton of his shirt. He stilled, shoulders hunched as he leaned his hands on the edge of the sink. The warmth of his skin flowed through her fingers and she wanted to put her cheek there and rest against the solid pillar of him.

He turned into her, and she dropped her hand from his back to his hip. He bent his head, touching his forehead to hers, and she felt his breath moving across her cheek. But just as she was getting light-headed again in anticipation, he straightened up and dropped a dry, whispering kiss to her forehead.

'Do you need a lift home?' he said.

She stepped back, her skirts flowing around her ankles.

'It's ok. I've got my car.'

16

The most frightened Griff had ever been in his life was when he was eighteen years old, and Mia nearly died.

It was the week he had his A Level results, and he'd been offered a place at his first-choice university: Edinburgh, to study History. Waverley had invited him and Mia to dinner to celebrate, and had taken them to a restaurant where he ordered champagne and lobster, insisting it was time Griff tried it now he was going to be a Man of the World. Griff shuddered to think how much it had cost.

Mia was giddy and over-excited all evening, most likely quite self-conscious in her New Look dress and bare legs at the posh restaurant. Griff wore the suit Waverley had bought him for university interviews.

Mia was always deferential to Waverley and obedient to any suggestion of his. She copied his behaviour at the restaurant, paying attention to his etiquette and the gentlemanly way he spoke to the staff. At the end of the evening, when they got out of the taxi back at Hartley, she gave Waverley a hug, and when he lay a fatherly hand on the top of her head, she seemed delighted, like a kitten snuggling into its owner's petting touch.

Griff shook Waverley's hand in a manly fashion. Since finishing school — or maybe since losing his mother — he was very aware of his need to be an adult now, even if he wasn't quite sure what that meant or how to go about it.

Waverley pulled him into a bear hug, almost crushing him with the weight of his affection.

'Your mother would be so proud,' Waverley said, the sound of tears in his voice. And then one of his big hands domed around each of Griff's ears and Griff's head was turned this way and that as Waverley kissed him on each cheek.

'There is always a home for you here,' Waverley said. 'You are never alone in the world. Remember that.'

Griff could only nod, determined not to cry.

Waverley said goodnight and headed into the house. Griff turned to Mia and saw the wistful expression on her face. To say Mia had issues with her own father was an understatement. But then she grinned, in that lightning way of hers.

'You're not ready to end the evening yet, are you?' she said.

He raised an eyebrow. 'What did you have in mind?'

What Mia had in mind was a midnight swim.

It was an evening not unlike the evening Griff had spent star-gazing with Lizzie: warm and clear. In the cove the waves were gentle and Mia slipped off her sandals to wade in, and then threw off her dress and tossed it to the shore.

Griff — behind her, fumbling with his jacket, wanting to take care of it — laughed but called a warning. 'Slow down! Don't go too far — you've been drinking!'

Her own laughter answered him, and the splash of her arms making strokes through the water.

'I'm going to swim away!' she called. 'I'm going to swim to France. You don't need me any more.'

Griff felt a shiver. He knew her well enough to recognise the undercurrents in her light mood. 'Don't be stupid!'

'You're leaving, you'll forget me! So goodbye . . . Goodbye . . . '

He kicked off his shoes. The waves sucked at the sand under his feet. Mia was a fair way out already.

'Mia, stop it, it's not funny.'

He bent to put aside his trousers, and by the time he looked out over the sea again, there was no sign of her.

He couldn't say, later, how much time passed while he waded and dived and reached blindly through the water, searching for her. Rationally, it couldn't have been very long; she was still breathing when he eventually found her and wrenched her to the surface. But it felt like hours. They were both exhausted.

He dragged her to the shore and she lay on the sand, crying from the shock of it. Griff knelt beside her.

'I didn't mean it,' she sobbed.

'I know . . .'

'I got a stitch in my side — it was so quick — I didn't mean it.'

'Hush, it's ok.' He pulled her into his arms and rocked her gently. Her wet hair was bedraggled across her shoulders like seaweed. At night-time, in the cooler air, a person smelled different coming in from the sea than they did in the sun.

She gulped a few times, like a distraught child.

'You're leaving me,' she wailed.

'I'm not.'

'You are. Even if you don't know it.'

There were weeks yet before he'd have to leave for university, but he couldn't pretend he didn't know what she meant. He hadn't really needed choose a place to study so far away, but his flat was full of grief and he just wanted to put some distance between him and the past. And yet, at the same time, he dreaded leaving

Mia as much as she dreaded him going.

'What if it's too much?' she said. 'What if I need you? What will I do?'

He took her face in his hands, the same way Waverley had held him, and said earnestly, 'You are never alone in the world. I promise. I promise you will always have me on your side.'

Slowly she calmed down. He wrapped her in his jacket. The suit — his first suit — was never the same once the lining had been wetted by salt water.

He kept his arm around her as they walked back to the house, and they fell asleep on the sofa, still damp from the sea, and still entwined.

When he left for university at the end of the summer, she waved him off. She hadn't wanted him to go. But though he felt sad, watching her shrink in the distance as the train pulled away from the platform, there was a kind of relief too.

Mia was right: they grew apart while he was away, and things were never quite the same between them. Still, when they eventually broke up, he thought he might die from it.

They lost contact for a couple of years, when she was moving around a lot, and when she came back into his life, she had Oscar. There was never again that level of intensity there had been during that summer. Griff was good for Mia; he was grounded, stabilising, an anchor. But in return she pulled him completely off kilter.

Once, he would have known exactly what she was thinking. But she was being so evasive right now he could only imagine. And from the few hints she had given him of her plans, he didn't like the impression he was getting. There was a reason she was still here, and it was to do with Oscar, and if it was her intention to convince Oscar to go with her when she left, Griff didn't know how he would handle that. He didn't want to make the child a prize in a tug of war.

It was nearly two a.m. when Lizzie went home, leaving Griff alone in the restaurant. His head was thumping, and he tried not to think about how unsubtly he had turned her away when she'd tried to comfort him. Instead, he went into his office and took up the pile of job applications Waverley had left with him earlier.

It had to be done. He had promised.

17

A journalist and a photographer from the local paper came to interview the theatre company the next morning. Lizzie was glad she wasn't expected to be in the photos, which were of the cast in full costume, because despite catching the sun over the last few days, she was looking washed out.

Meredith noticed. 'Are you feeling all right?' she asked Lizzie as they were getting ready to leave home that morning.

'Just a little tired.' 'Well, if you will stay out all night . . . ' Meredith teased. 'I think you're looking bright enough for the both of us,' Lizzie said.

Meredith smiled smugly. Jerome had given her a lift home after the dinner last night, and Meredith was obviously hopeful about the way things were developing between them. She sang along with the radio all the way to Hartley, drawing even more attention than usual from the cars pulling up next to their open windows, and pedestrians crossing in front of them.

'Have a wonderful day!' Meredith called to anyone who glanced her way.

'You're insufferable,' Lizzie said, but laughing.

By the time they arrived at Hartley, Lizzie felt more uplifted.

The journalist, Sally, was someone Lizzie had been at school with, and though she hadn't seen her in years, their conversation was easy and friendly and ended with plans to meet up in a few weeks for coffee, and Sally buying two of the few remaining tickets for the opening night.

Before she left, Lizzie shyly asked her for a favour, taking advantage of Sally's access to the newspaper's archives.

'Sure,' Sally said, when Lizzie made her request. 'I'll see what I can do.'

Lizzie wasn't sure quite what she was hoping for from Sally's search on the history of Hartley. At the same time, Fatima was struggling with her research into Victoria's soldier.

'The problem is,' she'd told Lizzie, 'without knowing his regiment, it's hard to find any service records.'

Lizzie didn't know what to try next. She was blundering around in the dark, and she was aware of time growing short. Not so much because her time at Hartley was running out, but because she was afraid of what Victoria might try next to get her attention.

While the others were having their photos taken for the newspaper article, Lizzie sneaked down to the cove.

The mouth of the smugglers' tunnel wasn't so forbidding in the daylight, but as Lizzie stood at the entrance, she was aware she was in the same spot where she had seen Victoria standing the night before, and it made her shiver. She couldn't help looking at the sand for footprints. The coarse sand was scuffed and uneven, but it gave nothing away.

She tried to remember how Victoria had been standing and where she had been pointing, and peered into the gloom of the opening.

Gathering her courage, she took a few steps inside. It was immediately much cooler. The air smelled of salt and seaweed and the sand was damp under her feet. It was astonishing how quickly the light disappeared, unable to penetrate beyond the first few meters. The tunnel was narrow, and became even more so as it travelled inwards, and between the dark, the unmoving air, and the close rock, Lizzie quickly felt claustrophobic and had to turn back.

The smugglers, she imagined, must have set torches along the route. Even then, she wouldn't like to travel it alone.

Before she left, as her vision adjusted, she saw evidence of a campfire not far in from the entrance: a circle of stones surrounding charred driftwood and ashes. So someone must have found it comfortable enough to use for shelter. Or been desperate.

Lizzie stepped back to the lit mouth of the tunnel, but she didn't leave. Her unease could have had a hundred different causes; it could have been just her over-active imagination that was leading her to fancy another presence in the tunnel with her. Whatever it was, she felt again that she wasn't alone.

'If you wanted my attention,' she said loudly, 'you've got it.' She paused. Mouth dry, heart racing.

'I'm listening,' she called.

Immediately she felt foolish. What was she expecting to happen?

But she reminded herself that she hadn't imagined what she'd seen last night. She hadn't made up Griff's injury. You could see the boat now, collapsed in its petrified state, tilted on its side on its buttress of sand, where for months — years — before, it had been wedged on stable foundations. She took a long breath and persisted.

'Tell me how to help you,' she said clearly to the empty beach, the cloudless sky, the dark shadows.

A gull cried as it flew overhead. As the sound died away, she thought she heard another noise, this time coming from inside the rock.

Breathy laughter. Deep. Malicious.

It echoed through the tunnel.

Lizzie backed away in horror. She couldn't be brave; she turned and fled across the beach and back to the house, hurrying the whole way.

★ ★ ★

As soon as she saw her friends eating lunch on the lawn, she felt a little better, but she didn't join them right away. Instead she slipped inside the summerhouse, where she could have some quiet to gather herself.

She hid herself deep among the costumes and props, careful to make sure that she could still hear her friends' voices, so she could know she wasn't really alone.

Gradually she calmed down. Her thoughts cleared and she was able to start untangling them. That wasn't Victoria.

She was so obscured in her hiding

place that when Oscar came in, he didn't notice her. He went to the table, his back to her. She pushed aside a hanger on a rail to let him know she was there, and he jumped, startled.

'Hey,' Lizzie said. 'What are you up to?'

It was an innocent question, but Oscar flushed and put his hands behind his back. 'Nothing.'

Frowning, Lizzie peered around him, and saw the piece of costume jewellery that had gone missing a week ago, now on the table.

'I found it,' Oscar said.

'Oh. Good.' She didn't want to make the poor kid uncomfortable, but she had to know. 'I thought perhaps your mum may have picked it up by accident when she was last here . . . ?'

He glanced at her quickly, then away again, and Lizzie knew she was right about Mia having it. Gently, she said, 'Thank you for bringing it back.'

Oscar fidgeted, still looking uncomfortable.

Lizzie leaned back against the table, half sitting on it. 'Did Griff tell you what happened last night?'

'He said he fell over in the boat. He's got a big bruise, here.' Oscar pointed to his own forehead.

'Is he ok?'

'I made him breakfast.'

She smiled. 'I'm sure that helped.'

'I'll look after him.'

Lizzie tilted her head. That was definitely something he'd got from Griff: taking the weight of the world on his shoulders. As she watched him, Oscar nudged the necklace onto the table, nibbling on the fingertips of his other hand.

'What's wrong?' Lizzie asked.

'Do you think Griff would be all right on his own?'

Lizzie flexed her grip on the edge of the table. She recognised how important it was to find the right words to answer him.

'Are you going somewhere?'

He shrugged. 'Maybe.'

'With your mum, do you mean?'

Oscar shrugged again.

'Has she said something to you about leaving?'

'I don't know,' he mumbled. 'She says she needs me and she wishes I could come with her . . .'

'You don't have to, if you don't want to.'

Oscar looked at her sharply. 'Yes, I do. She's my mum. I have to take care of her.'

Lizzie's heart twisted. 'No, love,' she said carefully. 'It's the other way around.'

Oscar's face was fierce, half angry with defensiveness on his mother's behalf, but half hopeful too. Lizzie wanted to give him a hug, but he was so full of bristling pride that she didn't want to patronise him.

'Have you talked to Griff about this?' she said.

'No. Don't say anything.'

'All right. But only if you promise me that if you're thinking of going with your mum, you'll talk to Griff first.'

Oscar thought about it for a moment,

and then nodded. If he was using Griff as a role model, Lizzie knew she could trust him to keep his word, and she relaxed a little.

'What were you doing in here when I came in?' Oscar asked eventually. 'I didn't see you.'

'Hiding,' Lizzie said. 'Sometimes I need a break from the world.'

Oscar looked around. It was quiet in the summerhouse, full of sunshine and the smell of makeup and powders.

'Can I have a break with you?' he asked.

She couldn't help it, she hugged him to her and kissed the top of his head. He put his arms around her waist, his cheek against her middle.

'Course you can. But only for a few minutes. Then we've got to be brave and face the world.'

* * *

When she got home that night, she found an email from her journalist friend. It contained attachments of the articles Sally had found in the newspaper archives.

The first was Victoria's husband Clifford's obituary. He had outlived Victoria by thirty years and had remarried after her death, leaving Hartley to live elsewhere. He had left quite a large family in the end, but otherwise his obituary was unremarkable.

The second attachment from Sally was Steven Grey's obituary, from 1907. Victoria's father had died of a heart attack while at the races one Saturday afternoon.

The writer spoke about Mr Grey as a shipowner and landowner, his position in society and his family connections. The wife and daughter he left behind. The article mentioned Hartley and the parties it was known for, and Mr Grey's gregariousness and booming voice, which somehow — very subtly — led into talking about his tendency to sail close to the wind and the trouble he'd got himself into once or twice with His Majesty's Revenue officials — which was somehow all forgotten in light of his generous donations and patronage . . .

It was all very oblique and well-mannered, but clear enough: Steven Grey was known for bribery and shady business practices. Apparently, it wasn't such a secret history after all.

That certainly hadn't been in the scrapbooks.

Lizzie wrote a reply to Sally to thank her for her help. Then she lay awake most of the night, thinking.

She had a sense of Victoria's father now. She had an idea of Victoria. But Thomas Madden was a shapeless blur.

Had he been involved with Victoria's father's business? Had he wilfully or reluctantly left her? Why had Victoria never been able to get over him?

Maybe it wasn't complicated at all. Maybe Thomas had simply never cared for Victoria.

When Lizzie finally did get to sleep, she had a disturbing dream.

She was back on the beach, where she'd been with Griff on Monday. But this time she was alone in the little rowboat. It shifted and lurched under her feet as if she was on stormy waters, until she was afraid she'd be tossed overboard into the shark-infested sea.

And then, just as she lost her footing and began to fall, Griff's hand was reaching towards her. She stretched to clasp it — but her hand passed right through his ghostly grip.

She tensed, preparing herself for a hard landing, but instead of striking water, or rock, or the corner of the wooden boat, she found herself upright again, standing outside the tunnel. Standing where Victoria had been standing.

She was still Lizzie, but she was Victoria too. When her thoughts came, she didn't know if they were hers or Victoria's.

I could be standing here for all eternity.

There was something terrible in the tunnel. Lizzie couldn't leave or move away; Victoria wouldn't let her. There was a reason to stay. There was a reason to be there.

* * *

Lizzie woke to a pounding on her door that in her dream had been something knocking from within the rock of the tunnel.

'Come on, slowcoach!' Meredith called from outside. 'Did you sleep through your alarm again?'

Lizzie propped herself up on her elbows. Dress rehearsal day, she remembered, with a twist of panic in her guts.

Was that why she was feeling so anxious?

No. It was a hangover from the dream. And even after a shower, and breakfast, and walking out into the sun-bleached day to the car, she couldn't shake it.

* * *

She made two visits that morning: the first was to the pear tree outside Griff's window. The tree that wasn't a tree.

Even without knowing its history she would have been able to tell there was something strange about it today. There wasn't a leaf on it. Its branches looked delicate and forlorn.

Lizzie came to stand underneath it and, as she had done before, put her hand gently to its trunk.

'Well,' she whispered, 'you're not scary at all, are you?'

Griff was right: it was friendly. She felt she was in company. It gave her courage; it meant ghosts didn't necessarily mean harm.

She knew she had to go back to the tunnel, but she couldn't quite bring herself to do it. The feelings that the dream had brought up kept returning to her, along with images of the darkness too, and she was unsettled and distracted all morning. So instead of going back to the beach, she made the folly her second destination that morning.

Griff had explained that this was the place where the tunnel emerged, from where the smugglers carried their loot on into town. Perhaps, away from the booming sea, the tunnel would be less echoing and creepy.

She rounded the folly, taking the stone steps down to its foundations, where the shrubs grew thicker and more wild. The pathway was narrow and overgrown. Even a hundred years ago any figures using it would have been concealed, nothing but shadows in the moonlight.

She expected it to be so overgrown from lack of use that it might not be possible to pass, but as far as she could tell, the way in wasn't blocked.

She had no chance to explore, however, because she was disturbed by a stranger.

He had approached from behind her while she was peering into the tunnel, and when he spoke, the sound of his voice so nearby made her nearly jump out of her skin.

'Something interesting in there?' he said.

She spun around, holding a hand over her hammering heart, and saw the man, tall and lean in jeans, with short, untidy hair and stubble.

'Sorry,' he said with a half-smile. 'Didn't mean to startle you.'

Lizzie backed away from the tunnel and reflexively back into the light.

'That's ok,' she said, laughing at herself.

He threw the stub of a cigarette he'd been smoking carelessly onto the path.

'You're not a tenant here,' she said.

He gave her a charming smile, fixing his gaze on her. He was quite handsome, she supposed; although the fact that he was so willing to use his handsomeness made him somewhat less attractive to her.

'Actually, no.'

She hesitated. Did she have a right to question him about his presence?

'I'm here to see a friend of mine,' he said. 'She's visiting her little boy. I'm just not sure which apartment . . .'

He trailed off, inviting her to leap in with assistance.

Rather than give him any information, she said, 'You're quite a long way from the apartments.'

The man's smile slid off his face. Lizzie felt the chill of his displeasure. She took another step back.

'I'm sorry, I can't help you,' she said.

'I just thought I'd have a look around. Didn't mean to intrude,' he said affably, spreading his hands.

Lizzie hurried up the steps. The man followed. She felt a burst of relief when she came out at the top and saw Griff standing beside the folly.

'Hi, I was wondering where you were!' Griff's gaze followed her gaze as she glanced back over her shoulder, and he saw the man stop midway on the steps behind her.

'Can I help you?' Griff asked the man, icily polite.

Lizzie went to him, feeling better for having him there, and he must have picked up on her uncertainty because he nudged an inch in front of her protectively.

'I was just saying,' the man said, back

188

to his charming smile, 'I'm here to visit a friend of mine. Trying to track down the right apartment.'

'I know all the tenants,' Griff said. 'Perhaps I can help.'

'Her name is Mia. She's visiting her son, Oscar.'

'Sorry, I think you've made a mistake.'

The man came to the top of the steps. He was taller and broader than Griff.

'No, I'm pretty sure this is the place,' he said, his eyes scanning the garden.

'Oscar's staying with me. We haven't seen Mia.'

The man appraised him. 'Oh, so you're the one . . .'

'How do you know Mia?'

The man paused, hooking his thumbs in his pockets, and then clearly decided it wasn't necessary for him to answer.

'If you do see her,' he said, 'will you tell her Adam's looking for her? She'll know what it's about.'

Griff pointed towards the main entrance of the house. 'The way out is that way.'

The man smirked and made a slight, sarcastic bow. But he headed in the way Griff indicated, soon disappearing from sight.

Lizzie took Griff's arm. He seemed calm enough, but she could feel the tension in him.

'It wasn't just me that found him creepy, then?' she muttered.

He gave her hand a squeeze but then — very deliberately, she thought — untangled himself from her.

'What did he say to you?' he asked.

'Only that he was here to see Mia.'

'Did you tell him anything?'

Lizzie shook her head. 'It's Mia's business if she doesn't want to be found.'

Griff gazed after the man, scratching his chin.

'Did you want me?' Lizzie said.

'Hmm?'

'You were looking for me?'

He turned back to her, his expression grave. The bruise was dark and lumpish on his forehead, the rest of his face colourless.

'It doesn't matter now,' he said.

'Can we . . . catch up later? No, wait, I've got a run-through . . . '

'I've got a busy evening at the restaurant.'

'Griff . . . '

She felt a distance growing between them and wondered if he was too distracted even to be aware of it. Was their evening on the beach, and all the closeness between them, just a one-off?

He nodded towards the lawn to warn her that someone was coming. She turned and saw Meredith marching towards them. Her sister impatiently started talking from so far away Lizzie didn't even catch her first words. She got the general impression, though; helped by Meredith's scowl and the emphaticn nature of her step.

' . . . you keep disappearing like this?' Meredith was saying when she caught up with them. 'You know how much we've got to do today. Or have you forgotten what your job is?'

Lizzie had a certain amount of

tolerance for Meredith's irritation, knowing how much pressure she was under. And she was right: Lizzie shouldn't have disappeared. Still, she was surprised by her sister's tone.

'I'm coming now,' Lizzie said.

'Get it together, Liz. Or do you expect me to do everything?'

Griff raised an eyebrow at Lizzie, and then took a gentlemanly step back, raising his hand in a tactful goodbye. Lizzie was embarrassed. 'Mer . . . '

'The props are a mess. We've lost the camera. You're the props manager — nothing's going to run smoothly if we can't find anything!'

Griff had started to leave, but now he stopped and turned back.

'Sorry — you've lost your camera?'

'It was there last night,' Lizzie said. 'I checked.'

'Well, things have a habit of going missing in chaos,' Meredith said, her hands on her waist.

Griff caught Lizzie's eye once more before leaving her alone with Meredith.

'I'm coming, I'll sort it out,' Lizzie said to her sister. 'You didn't have to be rude in front of Griff.'

Meredith opened her mouth and Lizzie expected a bad-tempered tirade, but Meredith stopped herself.

'All right. Sorry. But let's go, can we?' She started walking, leading Lizzie back towards the summerhouse. 'Seriously, Lizzie, you're never where you're supposed to be these days. You know this rehearsal is important. My agent is coming.'

Lizzie didn't speak for a few minutes, letting Meredith's ire blow out, but before they got back to the others, she said gently, 'Is there something else wrong?'

Meredith stopped walking. She sighed and dipped her head, combing her fingers through her loose hair.

'Jerome's not answering my texts.'

'Oh.'

'I think he's worried about the amount of time I spend away travelling. Or something. I don't know. He's not the easiest to talk to.'

'How many texts have you sent him?'

'Two.'

'Two? Since the other night?'

'I don't want to inundate him. You know he's not the chatty kind.'

'Apparently you're not either, when it comes to him. I'd risk one more text. Maybe even a call. He doesn't seem like the kind to ghost a girl.'

'That's what I thought,' Meredith said, setting off again. 'But we can be wrong about these things.'

18

When Griff came home, he found Mia curled up asleep on the sofa in a patch of sunshine, like a cat.

He took a pile of books off the coffee table and dropped them on to the floor with a bang. He should be at the bank right now; he had wanted to invite Lizzie to have lunch with him afterwards. He begrudged Mia for derailing his plans for the day — again.

Mia woke yawningly. 'What's going on?'

'That's what I want to know.'

He sat down on the coffee table, leaning forward, elbows on knees so he could pin her with his gaze.

'Who's Adam?' he said.

The sleepiness vanished from Mia and she sat up. 'Why are you asking?' 'I just met him downstairs. He's looking for you.'

'Did you tell him . . . ?'

They both turned as Oscar appeared in his bedroom doorway. His face was stricken, and Griff cursed himself for not thinking of checking where he was before confronting Mia.

Before he could say anything, Mia stretched a hand out to Oscar. 'Come here. Come here, kid. It's ok.'

Oscar didn't move. Not until Griff said, 'Of course I didn't tell him anything. He left; he's gone now.'

Oscar sat beside Mia and she hugged him close to her side.

'Tell me,' Griff said.

'He's an old boyfriend. And yes, he's the one I've been avoiding. It was over between us a long time ago, before you took Oscar in, even.'

Griff winced to think of Adam being around Oscar.

'I guess he feels I still owe him something,' Mia went on. 'I heard he was back . . . He's been away on a short custodial sentence.' She could barely meet Griff's eye as she said it. 'That's why I decided now was the time to try some place new. I never meant to stay here so long.' Now she glanced at Griff appealingly. 'I felt safe here, and I kept putting it off . . .'

'You should have told me,' Griff said.

'I know. But I didn't think it would be an issue. How did I know he'd find me?'

'What was he arrested for?'

'Handling stolen goods.'

Griff was quiet, struggling with his anger. There was no point getting cross with Mia; she shrank away from it and turned into something impossible.

Eventually, he said, 'I think you should go, Mia.'

He wanted to add that she should never have stayed so long and risked getting Oscar caught up in it, but from her sheepish expression she probably understood that. There were a million things he wanted to say — none of which he could, in front of Oscar.

'Get in touch with your friend,' he said, 'tell her you're on your way. I'll buy you a train ticket.'

She'd need money too. Mentally, he

started adding up how much cash he could spare.

'There's something else,' she said. 'Another reason I came.' She turned to Oscar, put her hands on his shoulders and looked at him seriously. 'You know what it is, O?'

Griff thought he'd been tense before, but now he felt the room spin with real fear. She couldn't really mean to . . . ?

Oscar glanced at him, wide-eyed, his freckles stark on his pale face. Griff sat on his hands to resist the urge to snatch him from his mother.

'I don't know,' Oscar whispered.

'The thing I gave you,' she prompted. 'The treasure.'

Oscar's eyes darted to Griff again, and Griff saw his own confusion mirrored on Oscar's face.

'Did you bury it like I told you?' she said.

Realisation altered Oscar's expression. 'I thought . . . ' he said.

'What?'

'Didn't you come to get me? Don't

you want me to come with you?'

What was worse: being asked to leave with her, or not being asked?

He was a child; as soon as he realised he could stay in his home, he was devastated about being left behind.

'Oh, love, of course I do!' Mia said. She pulled him into a tight hug. 'I'm just not sure it's such a good idea right now. One day we'll be together again. When I'm settled. Soon. I promise.'

Griff watched Oscar carefully, ready for his own heart to break if Oscar's did. But from his mum's arms, Oscar looked at Griff, and the thing Griff

saw most was relief. He recognised it because it was the thing he was felling most just then too.

* * *

'This Adam guy,' Griff asked Mia quietly as they followed Oscar out of the house, and Griff found himself heading back towards the folly. 'Is he dangerous?'

Mia checked to make sure Oscar was

out of hearing.

'Not if he gets what he wants,' she muttered.

The idea that Mia had given Oscar something precious to look after so Adam wouldn't get his hands on it, and actually told him to bury it where no one would find it, was preposterous. But of course it was exactly the kind of thing Mia would do.

'What is it?' Griff asked. 'A family heirloom?'

'Something like that. I've had it since I was a teenager. It's worth enough to set me up and keep me going for a while.'

She looked at Griff, and read his mood from his stony features.

'I wouldn't put Oscar in danger for the world,' she said. 'You know that.'

She wouldn't. Not intentionally.

Griff rubbed his hand over his face with a sigh, and Mia sidled closer to him, bumping against him as they walked. 'Don't be angry with me.'

He didn't respond. By the time they caught up with Oscar at the folly, Oscar

200

was at the bottom of the steps.

'I buried it here,' Oscar said.

He took up a large flat stone with a sharp edge, and used it to scrape away the moss and ivy that had overgrown the small pocket at the base of the foundations where he had buried his treasure on the day he moved in to Hartley House.

A few moments later he drew out a grubby Nutella jar. Griff and Mia watched as he wiped the mud off by rubbing the jar on the grass.

'Clever boy,' Mia said. 'Let me see.'

She took the jar from him and twisted the lid off. Inside was a small piece of red felt, but as she held it between her fingertips, her brow knotted. She unfolded it; found it empty. Looked into the bottom of the glass jar; looked dumbly at her feet as if she might have dropped something without noticing.

'Where is it?' she asked Oscar.

'It's there,' he said.

'It's not.'

His expression turned anxious. 'I didn't touch it, I just buried it like you told me to.'

'You didn't open it — not even to have a look?'

Oscar shook his head vehemently.

'Then where is it?' she demanded.

'Mia,' Griff warned.

'I didn't touch it,' Oscar insisted.

Mia stopped, drew breath. 'Then someone else must have. Who else knew it was here?'

'No one. You told me not to tell anyone.'

'So no one knew? No one at all?'

Oscar hesitated. His eyes darted to Griff.

'What is it, O?' Griff said gently.

'Lizzie saw me, the day I buried it. But she didn't know what was inside — '

Mia was off, leaping up the steps. Oscar hurried to Griff. 'Don't let her shout at Lizzie.'

Griff touched Oscar's head, forced a smile. 'Don't worry, I'll keep an eye on her. You go and find Claudette at the restaurant — tell her I'll be back in a bit and ask her for some chocolate brownies while you wait, ok?'

Oscar hesitated uncertainly.

'It's all right, O. I'll take care of it. I promise.'

Oscar nodded. He went up the steps ahead of Griff and Griff watched him run off towards the restaurant before he hurried to catch up with Mia, full of trepidation.

Mia had interrupted Lizzie in the middle of work. When Griff reached them, Lizzie was leading Mia away from the stage for some privacy, while the rest of the company looked on without hiding their curiosity. Mia and Lizzie stood on a patch of lawn, Lizzie squinting in the sun and Mia pulling long strands of loose hair back from her face that were caught on the breeze.

'What's this about?' Lizzie asked Mia warily.

'An emerald ring. A square-cut emerald ring — vintage — a family heirloom.'

Lizzie glanced at Griff, who stopped beside them, out of breath. Her eyes in the sunlight were almost transparent.

'I don't understand.'

Mia held up the jar, with its scrap of felt jiggling stiffly inside.

'You saw Oscar bury it, didn't you?' she said.

'I saw Oscar bury something, months ago,' Lizzie said. She still looked perplexed.

'Well, it's gone now. And you're the only one who knew it was there.'

Understanding crossed Lizzie's face, and then disbelief. And then something Griff hadn't seen on Lizzie before: anger.

Amazing how Mia managed to bring it out in people.

'An emerald ring,' Lizzie said slowly.

'You must have it.'

'Mia,' Griff warned.

Lizzie stared hard at Mia. She seemed about to say something, and then bit her tongue. Her lips pressed together; her mouth flattened. Griff could imagine exactly what was on her mind. Eventually, jaw tight, she simply said, 'I'm not a thief.'

'What's that supposed to mean?' Mia

shot back defensively.

'Just what I said.'

'I want my ring!'

Griff stepped in now, putting himself between them, forcing Mia back a step. He placed his hands on Mia's upper arms to hold her there, and as he did, he noticed Oscar on the gravel path to the house, watching. 'Enough, Mia.'

'She took it — it's the only possible explanation.'

She wouldn't calm down. Oscar was dancing from foot to foot; Griff could tell he was getting upset and would soon come over to try and placate his mother.

Griff squeezed Mia's arms slightly. 'Please, Mia.'

'Whose side are you on?' she demanded.

He was aware of Oscar, impatiently trusting him to resolve the situation. He was even more aware of Lizzie, although his back was to her, as she waited for his response. Mia held his gaze challengingly. There was only one thing he could say.

'Yours,' he said to Mia. 'Always.'

He kept his eyes on Mia, felt her soften under his grip as the fire went out of her.

'Come on,' he said. 'Oscar's behind you.'

She made a show of being reluctant to drop the issue, but he knew she would now, for his sake. She started towards Oscar, and Oscar gave a relieved smile. Eventually, Griff turned back to Lizzie.

Lizzie was gone; already heading back to her workmates, away from him, her head tilted high. She didn't look back.

His heart plunged with the knowledge of what he had done.

19

Lizzie tried to immerse herself in her work. She was determined to do a good job. Before the dress rehearsal all the props and costumes had to be in perfect order. The cast had to have their make-up ready where they needed it; the props needed to be available on the right side of the stage when they reached for them.

She didn't join her friends for dinner at the restaurant, but chose to stay behind to make sure everything was set up ready for the show.

'Honey,' Daniel said, putting his arm around Lizzie's shoulders and bowing his head to rest on hers, 'there's plenty of time, and you're doing a great job. Meredith always turns into the Grinch before opening night — don't take any notice. Come and have dinner with us.'

Lizzie patted his arm. Its weight was almost strangling her. That was how you knew Daniel was fond of you.

'Thanks for saying so,' she said. 'But really, I want to make sure everything's right.'

He looked at her for a long moment. 'Is this anything to do with a certain restaurateur who might be there?'

Lizzie was embarrassed. She'd always been terrible at hiding her feelings. She swallowed.

Again, the twist in her stomach when she remembered Griff's whispered 'Always' to Mia.

'A little,' she said, seeing no point in denying it.

Daniel smooshed her into a bear hug, but even that couldn't make her smile.

'I'll bring you back something good to eat,' he offered.

Once she was alone, Lizzie sat down on the stage, trying to find calm in the cloudless sky.

It's nearly over, she told herself. The play starts; the play finishes its run. Keep yourself busy. You may not even have to see him again . . .

It was unfair that she had to feel like this on what should have been one of the most exciting evenings of her life.

It was unfair that she'd been accused of theft, when Mia was the one —

No. Stop. Don't be bitter.

The necklace, the cigarette case, the camera.

But Mia had issues. It was Griff Lizzie was hurt by.

'Yours,' he'd said. 'Always.'

Just like Victoria's soldier. They promise you one thing . . .

No, be fair. Griff never made any promises. Not to her. He'd always been honest.

Sometimes they just choose someone else.

She was thinking about Victoria again, and as always when her mind was on Victoria, she imagined she could feel her presence. Victoria's frustration was thick in the air, mingling with Lizzie's emotions until she didn't know whose were whose.

Lizzie stood up. 'I don't know what

you expect me to do.'

There was a clatter behind her as the Queen of Hearts' croquet stick fell over from where it had been quite securely propped against the wall. Lizzie jumped away from it. But suddenly, more than frightened, she was annoyed, and fed up, and angry.

'There's nothing I can do!' she said, throwing the words into the air. 'I can't make him love you!'

The world fell still. Lizzie held her breath and gazed around. She knew there were people in the house, and at the restaurant, and probably in the different parts of the garden too, but she could see no one just then; there was no other living being in sight.

Uneasily, she went back to the summerhouse and let herself in. Daniel's Cheshire Cat make-up was lined up neatly on the table; Fatima's string of magicians' handkerchiefs hung from a peg. Lizzie felt guilty for saying such a mean-spirited thing to Victoria. But then she remembered the kick to her leg, and the tipping of the boat . . . And even as she did, she knew that Victoria wasn't going to let her get away with the comment.

She held her breath in anticipation.

She'd seen Victoria now, more than once. She'd spoken to her too. Victoria was acknowledged now; that meant she was strong.

Daniel's make-up was swept up off the table, flying through the air to strike the glass door with a crack. Lizzie flinched, ducking down, covering her head with her arms.

That was only the beginning of it.

She fled back out to the lawn, and could only watch as a storm of colour and noise played out in the summer-house, with costumes and props flying about with such fury that Lizzie was amazed none of the windows were broken.

It didn't last long, but she didn't wait. She ran to the side of the house, to where the pear tree stood, and threw herself down at the base of its trunk. In its leaflessness, the tree looked much as she felt: kind of vulnerable. Lizzie crooked her knees and put her head in her arms and cried. She let herself indulge in all the self-pity she could manage.

When all her emotion was burned out, she wiped her eyes on her sleeves and raised her head.

The cool shade of the tree had expanded as she'd sat beneath it, and now she saw why: shoots of new growth covered every branch of the tree in the vivid green of spring, and it seemed even as she watched that white blossom was beginning to appear.

She watched in wonder; even laughed a little. Then she put her hand to the trunk.

'Thank you,' she said.

* * *

Back at the summerhouse, Meredith was cursing at the mess, while Kate, Fatima and Daniel picked through the piles of clothes on the floor, rescuing what they recognised. The delicate caterpillar puppet, which was five feet tall and made of paper and wire, and which Lizzie had made herself months ago, was crumpled in the corner in a way that made Lizzie's chest hurt.

'What happened?' Meredith demanded when she saw Lizzie. 'Where have you been?'

'I'll sort it out,' Lizzie said, picking up one of Alice's shoes and searching for its pair.

'I don't understand . . . We've got thirty minutes, Lizzie.'

'It'll be ok,' Lizzie said, afraid to look at Meredith in case her sister read her recent crying bout on her face. 'I'll explain later.'

She lifted Meredith's Queen of Hearts dress and shook it out, relieved to see it wasn't damaged. She hung it on the rail, checking its position in the order of changes.

It was when she dropped her hand over the red felt hearts adorning the corset that she was struck by something that really should have occurred to her earlier: she was reminded of the ragged red felt that had wrapped Mia's missing ring, the only thing left in the glass jar when Oscar dug it up, and she remembered what was familiar about it, and where she had seen something like it before.

* * *

There was no time to think of it again that evening. The dress rehearsal started twenty minutes late. In the audience, Meredith's agent kept checking her watch, and the family and friends of the cast who had been invited fidgeted uncomfortably on their picnic blankets and folding chairs. It wasn't quite as Lizzie had hoped.

At one point during the interval she looked out and noticed Waverley in the audience. He gave her a cheery thumbs up, but all Lizzie could think was how the bucket seat he was sitting in couldn't be good for his sciatica.

'Well, this is a blimmin' disaster,' Kate

muttered, moving past Lizzie into the 'backstage' area.

The sheet onto which they projected Alice's shadow in the first act, to give the impression of her growing large and small when she drank the potion and ate the cake, had fallen down midway through the scene. Daniel had missed his cue to go on as the Cheshire Cat because he'd only just discovered his tail was falling off, and he had to wait for Lizzie to pin it back on. And they hadn't been able to fix the caterpillar in time, and so had to make do with the puppet sitting inanimately in the corner, where usually Fatima would be dancing it up and down.

Thank heaven for Meredith. When the Queen appeared after the interval, she pulled everything together. Meredith's charisma flooded the whole garden. No one could doubt her professionalism at least.

She wasn't talking to Lizzie, though.

'You know what they say,' Daniel said encouragingly to Lizzie when Meredith brushed past her after the final round of applause. 'Terrible dress rehearsal means a great opening night. We'll have all the kinks worked out by then.'

'Thanks, Daniel,' Lizzie said in a small voice. Shouldn't she be the one giving pep talks?

The applause, Lizzie felt, had been genuine. But then, the tickets had been free.

On the drive home, when they were stopped at a traffic light near the house, Meredith finally broke her punishing silence.

'So, are you going to tell me what happened?'

'There was a ghost in the summerhouse,' Lizzie said in a low voice, staring down at her lap.

'If it was too much for you, you should have told me,' Meredith said, managing to sound both annoyed and concerned at the same time.

'It's not too much.'

'Should I be worried about you, Liz?'

'No.' She glanced at Meredith. 'I'm fine.'

The car behind them tooted; Lizzie had missed the green light. She raised a hand in a conciliatory gesture and pulled away.

'There was a representative from an arts charity there this evening,' Meredith said. 'They were thinking of giving us a grant to tour. It was the only night he could come.'

Lizzie's stomach plummeted. 'Why didn't you tell me?'

'I didn't want to stress you out.'

'Meredith, I can take the responsibility — I want to — that's why I'm here!'

She pulled up outside their house and turned fully to Meredith.

'Did you speak to him? What did he say?'

'I'm not sure he was particularly impressed. He wished us luck.'

Even Lizzie knew that was code for polite rejection.

'Maybe it's for the best.' Meredith turned to the window. She'd scrubbed off all her make-up and she looked tired.

'What do you mean?'

But Meredith was distracted. Something she'd seen lit a small flame in her, making her eyes shine again: Jerome's van was parked across the road, and when he saw they had arrived, he stepped out of it and stood waiting for Meredith to join him.

Better than a text message.

'Mer,' Lizzie said, stopping her sister as she reached for the door handle. 'It'll be all right, honestly.'

Meredith paused but didn't answer.

'You were amazing tonight,' Lizzie added.

Finally, Meredith looked at her, gave her a sad smile.

'Let's all try and be amazing next time, eh?'

Lizzie watched her get out of the car and cross to Jerome. She stood in front of him a moment, and neither of them spoke. Lizzie knew Meredith was waiting for him to start first. It seemed she might be waiting a while.

Eventually Jerome said something short. Meredith nodded towards the house, and he followed her inside.

Lizzie stayed in the car to give them a few minutes privacy. She couldn't stand to see Meredith's disappointment in her. She knew it was because Meredith had as much invested in the play as she did, and didn't blame her. But it still hurt.

She had to make the opening night a success. She didn't care what she had to do to achieve it, but she needed to find a way to keep Victoria from sabotaging all their work. She had to find out what Victoria wanted.

20

The next day, Lizzie stood outside the summerhouse slowly turning a silver sixpence in her fingers. The coin had been in her make-up case that morning.

Surely it had appeared on the wrong day? Opening night wasn't until tomorrow.

She hadn't spoken to Meredith before she left home. She wouldn't have told her about the sixpence anyway; Meredith's tolerance for such things was low right now.

Meredith and Jerome had been in the kitchen when Lizzie let herself into the house last night. Meredith had been pouring tea, and Lizzie hadn't heard any conversation between them. She'd headed straight for the stairs when she came in, to give them space, carrying the caterpillar puppet from the boot of her car bundled carefully in her arms.

When she was halfway up the stairs,

she heard Jerome saying, in a perplexed way, 'Wait — how many texts am I supposed to send?' as if he couldn't quite understand modern communication.

Lizzie smiled to herself and continued up the stairs, and by the time she reached the top, there was laughter coming from the kitchen.

She closed herself in her bedroom, and stayed up until the early hours to fix the poor caterpillar.

In the morning she left early and went to the local greasy spoon café for breakfast. Over toast and tea, she checked her emails and the website, updating it to include a link to the article Sally had printed that day in the local paper. It was a nice piece, making the play sound fun and the ideal summer activity, while at the same time making a fuss of local celebrity Meredith Palmerstone, of the internationally famous voice.

Meredith was in the centre of the group photograph printed alongside the article, managing to look both regal and mad in her Queen of Hearts costume, while Fatima, Daniel and Kate surrounded her in various theatrical poses.

'Well, I'd buy a ticket,' Lizzie murmured quietly to herself.

She emailed Sally to thank her for writing such a positive article.

Next, she went to the printers to pick up the programmes. There had been a few problems with the initial layout — misspellings of cast names; Kate's head shot being printed in the space where Fatima's should have been . . . So Lizzie was relieved to see everything was perfect in these final copies.

Maybe her luck was changing.

By mid-morning she'd arrived at Hartley. The rest of the company, having worked late last night, were taking the morning off and would come in later. Lizzie was reluctant to go near the summerhouse by herself; as she approached it, she kept turning the coin in her fingers like a talisman.

She had no choice, really. The props could be in perfect order, the programmes stunning, and the website as attractive as could possibly be . . . none of it would matter if Victoria decided to disrupt things again.

She slipped the coin into the pocket of her jeans and steeled herself.

On her first day, when she'd climbed on to the roof of the summerhouse, she'd noticed that there was an easier way to get up there, and now she set out to find the route. She took the path away from the summerhouse, curving around its boundary, past the fish pond and the place where the pair of bantam chickens who belonged to the estate often took shelter in the shrubbery when the sun was too hot. Today it was breezy, and ripples fanned across the surface of the pond. Once past it, she came to the bank behind the summerhouse.

Its slope was steep, but manageable. Safer than a ladder, Lizzie felt, in the current climate.

She climbed up, wedging her toes into clumps of thick grass, using her hands to stabilise herself when she needed to, clambering like a monkey and not caring how ungainly she looked.

When she stepped onto the summer-house roof, she stopped to catch her breath. And listened.

It was hard to tell whether Victoria was around or not. Just in case, Lizzie said loudly, 'I'm here to help. I just want to find out the truth, ok?'

She really didn't want to face any more bouts of rage from Victoria. Very slowly, she approached the loose stone-work where she'd found the biscuit tin the last time. Carefully, respectfully, she drew it out again.

She sat cross-legged on the summer-house roof and opened the tin.

On the very top was the piece of aged red felt, just as she had left it — a piece identical to what Lizzie had seen inside the jar Oscar had buried, when Mia waved it at her. But the pocket of felt was no longer empty. Lizzie found a square-cut emerald ring tucked inside.

Her skin tingled as she set it aside, careful not even to touch the gold. She moved on to the stack of letters.

They were fragile in the folds, as though they had been packed and unpacked dozens of times, but although the ink had faded, the writing wasn't difficult to read. Angling herself so her back was to the sun, Lizzie lost herself in the letters.

The dates were vague. Rather than giving the month or year, the letters were simply marked 'Monday a.m.' or 'Sunday evening', as if notes had been passed so frequently between the couple, they didn't need to be grounded in any wider context. They were stacked in clear order, however: every letter that Lt Thomas Madden had written to Victoria Grey over their intense summer together. And Lizzie read them all.

I tried to resist, but you won't let me. I have no choice but to give myself over to you completely . . .

. . . You were beautiful last night in your peach dress, and I wanted to tell you a dozen times right there in the dining room, but you know that I can't . . .

. . . You say you want to be alone with me, but, my darling, it would not be wise. Next week I will be gone, and what will become of you? You know I have nothing to offer you. All my commitments are elsewhere . . . '

. . . Of course. A Million times, of course. But your father would never accept me . . .

If I live to be one hundred and ten, I will never forget the sight of you at your window in the candlelight, waiting for me. The dear pear tree outside, grown tall all of a sudden, as if it were building me a ladder to climb upon. I feel that tree is our best friend. I am not sure we have many others . . .

. . . You asked me if I am angry. I am, but not with you. Why shouldn't we be allowed to show our feelings without others behaving as if we have done something scandalous? Why must other people have so much power over us, and dictate the choices of our lives?

Time passed, and the stack of unread letters left by Lizzie's hand became slim.

I must go, before your father invites me to leave. It would by an insult to both of us to allow this situation to become any uglier in front of your other guests, who are all so keen to think badly of me. I will write to you, and I will do it in a thousand under-hand ways if I need to, to be sure my letters aren't stopped before they reach you. If you don't hear from me, it will be because my attempts have been thwarted. Never doubt that I am thinking of you constantly and planning for ways for us to be together. I meant the promise I made to you. I have left to you the one thing of value that I own: my mother's ring. One day I will return, and you can wear it openly, and we will make each other new promises. Have faith in me, Victoria. My heart is all for you.

A seagull landed on the rooftop near Lizzie with a squawk, startling her from her thoughts. She tossed a pebble in its direction, and it took flight again, spreading its huge white wings.

The last letter in the pile wasn't as worn as the others, and it was on different paper: pale blue. The ink was black and the handwriting emphatic.

Where are you? I have no address to send this letter, but I sit down to write it anyway, because I must do something to feel nearer to you. It has been ten days, and no news from you. My father thinks I should take this as proof of your character. I would like to think it was beneath him to keep your letters from me, but recently I begin to see him in a new light, and now I don't know what he might be capable of. I cannot forgive him for the way he treated you.

My cousin, Isabel, warned me of the damage gossip can do. I think it has already done its damage to you. She told me you were known to be a flirt. That you may be a rogue. I know what you are, and what you are not. I know you, and I know my heart, and if we two are alone in the world to know the truth, I don't care, as long as the truth is known by someone.

I am waiting for you. I have faith in you. And even as gossip begins to take its toll on my reputation, and everyone starts to look at me with different eyes, I don't care. I can bear anything as long as I see you again.

Lizzie's vision blurred behind tears. So it was love. Real, true love, on both sides. There could be no doubting it.

That was why Victoria was so furious with Lizzie. Lizzie had called Thomas a cad, accused him of not loving Victoria — accused him of taking her father's money to leave her, even.

But if he hadn't left Victoria willingly, why had he never come back for her?

At least the ring was back in its rightful place.

Lizzie knew Victoria's strength had been growing ever since Lizzie started taking notice of her, but it was still impressive that Victoria had been able to get to the ring, and bring it back here.

Mia must have found it in this tin too,

back in the days when she used to visit Hartley to see Griff, and would roam freely over the grounds. Lizzie already knew Mia was a thief, but it was shocking to think of her finding something so valuable and deciding to keep it for herself. The ring was beautiful, certainly, and must have been tempting, but it was very obviously not for the taking.

A cloud moved over the sun, giving Lizzie's eyes a rest from the bright glare of the paper, and for a few moments she closed her eyes and considered whether she should pass the ring on to Waverley. It was part of his family history, after all. But it seemed to her that it very definitely belonged to Victoria, for as long as she was around. And Victoria wanted it kept here.

She sat back on her hands, stretching her numb legs in front of her. As she looked out over the gardens, she saw Griff crossing in the direction of the summerhouse. Her heart gave the same hard thump of recognition and wonder that it gave every time she saw him, before a pang when she remembered the last time they'd spoken.

'Ok,' she whispered. She knew that Victoria was with her, that she was guarding her treasure. That she had allowed Lizzie to read her secrets, because she had some purpose for Lizzie to know them. 'I get it now . . .'

But what Victoria wanted Lizzie to do with the knowledge was still a mystery.

21

Griff went into the garden that morning in the hope of finding Lizzie. When he noticed a figure on the summerhouse roof, he knew it must be her, and he was so filled with apprehension that it took all his courage to keep moving towards her.

He was familiar with the path she must have taken to get up there, though he hadn't taken it himself for over a decade. By the time he reached her, also by climbing up the side of the hill, he was breathless and grass-stained.

'Would you mind if I joined you?' he said, hovering at the back of the roof.

'Of course,' she said. She covered the tin beside her with its lid, and then placed it on the other side of her, to make room for him to sit down.

He had never felt awkward with Lizzie before. She wasn't hostile, but she wasn't looking at him either, casting her gaze placidly over the view as she waited for him to say something.

He hooked his elbows around his knees, clasped his hands.

'Mia's leaving today,' he said. 'Oscar is with her now, waiting outside the house for the taxi. I thought I'd give them some privacy to say goodbye . . .'

He glanced at her. She was looking down, her gaze unfocussed, but her head was tilted towards him as she listened.

He wanted to tell her more. Tell her everything.

Last night, after asking Waverley to take Oscar for a while, he and Mia had a long-overdue talk that quickly became an argument. He gave her as much money as he could spare, but he worried it wasn't enough to keep her out of trouble. He confronted her with her irresponsibility, told her off for her bad behaviour in front of Lizzie and Oscar, and ended by accusing her of being a thief.

'I think perhaps you lost some things from the theatre company as a result of Mia's presence . . .' he said now to

Lizzie. He cleared his throat self-consciously. 'I know Meredith's cigarette case is important to her. Mia wouldn't admit she took it — she says she never left the flat. It's true, actually, she hardly ever did . . . But I know she's a thief. I do know that, Lizzie. And I'm sorry . . . ' He glanced at her again. 'I'm so very sorry that she accused you. Of course I don't believe that you took the ring.'

Lizzie turned away, towards the tin beside her. She seemed uncomfortable. He swallowed. He couldn't blame her for resenting him, but it made every part of his body hurt that she was so closed to him.

'I'll make it up to you, I promise,' he said. 'I'll pay you back for the things that went missing.'

Lizzie finally looked at him with those large and earnest eyes.

'You don't need to do that,' she said. 'It's not your responsibility.'

He shook his head. 'But it feels like it is. Mia has always been my responsibility.'

Again, he wished he could say more. He wanted to explain how he felt that responsibility had ended last night. Mia was finally asking too much of him.

The sense that he had betrayed Lizzie, and his regret over hurting her, put a new perspective on everything. He wished he could go back to that moment when he was standing between her and Mia, and give a different answer, make a different choice. But it was too late. All he could do now was take an enlightened look at his relationship with Mia and allow himself to say no more to all the trouble it was causing him.

'I can't be the one to solve all your problems all the time,' he'd said to Mia, his exasperation thick in his voice. 'I can't always save you!'

Mia had been throwing her belongings haphazardly into her rucksack, making a dramatic show of packing, and answering everything he said to her by being defensive and contradictory. Now she paused, stunned, and turned to him.

'But you promised you would,' she

said tremulously.

Griff's anger deflated. She looked so vulnerable and lost, and he was suddenly filled with self-doubt.

'Mia . . . ' He reached a hand towards her, but she jerked away from his touch. She fled to the bedroom, slamming the door behind her.

Griff stared at the door for a long time. He knew if he went after her he would probably find her crying, and then he would comfort her, and his resolve would soften . . . and they would go back to exactly the way things were before. And that meant he would have to sacrifice Lizzie.

Now Mia was leaving, and they hadn't reconciled. She had blanked him all morning, punishing him with silence and a cold shoulder. She hadn't even answered him when he said goodbye.

Maybe it was better like this. He would speak to her when she was settled in her new place and smooth things over. A day or two and Mia would be in an entirely changed mood. They would be friends again, but their relationship would be different. He would be free.

With Mia gone, he could concentrate on trying to put things right with Lizzie.

'I wanted to thank you,' he said to her. He could feel himself begin to blush. He never blushed. But he wasn't used to talking about his feelings, and he was aware he could be making a complete fool of himself.

'What for?' Lizzie said in surprise.

'Being patient. Being so good with Oscar. Coming here in the first place. Everything. Just . . . showing me things could be different. I was drowning, Lizzie.'

She met his eyes now, and they were so near to each other it was as if there was an electric current between them. Once he allowed himself to open himself up to his feelings, they overwhelmed him. It made his head swim. He knew that he shone with hope, that he was utterly transparent, but he didn't care. Lizzie was brave enough to live her whole life like this, never hiding her feelings. She was astonishing.

Suddenly, she turned away, her brow creasing. Her hand dropped to the tin beside her.

'But what if I told you I did have the ring?' she said quietly.

'The ring?'

'The emerald ring that went missing after Oscar buried it,' she gently reminded him.

He shook the befuddlement from his head. 'Do you?'

'Kind of. I mean, I know where it is.'

'How?'

She took a breath. 'Victoria's ghost took it because it belonged to her; Thomas proposed with it before he left, and Victoria buried it up here with his love letters after he disappeared and she was pushed into marriage with someone else.'

She spoke very fast and watched him all the while. He took a moment to process what she was telling him. It sounded ridiculous, totally against all logic.

'So . . . You're telling me Mia stole it

from Victoria in the first place?'

She nodded, biting her lip.

'Wow. No wonder Victoria was cross,' he said.

Lizzie's smile was so huge he felt he could take off and fly. She looked like she wanted to kiss him. And so she did, pressing forward, touching her lips to his, a hard, fierce, passionate kiss that zapped electricity to his fingertips and left him dazed.

'So, am I forgiven?' he whispered.

'The moment you came looking for me,' she said.

22

He believed her about the ring. Griff always believed her. As soon as Lizzie heard that, she couldn't help showing her joy. And when she saw Griff's answering smile, so rare a thing, she found it irresistible. A kiss was the only possible response.

It seemed to surprise both of them. Immediately after, she drew back in shyness, touching her fingertips to her mouth. She saw Griff's amused half-smile from the corner of her eye.

Nonchalantly, she flipped her sunglasses down from the top of her head to cover her eyes and some of her burning cheeks. Griff chuckled. He curled a teasing finger around the arm of the sunglasses where they hooked behind her ear, and the intimacy of the touch made her shiver.

'Can I see?' he said. 'The ring?'

She lifted the tin and handed it to him, trying to attune herself again to Victoria's presence, to discern whether she would mind Griff having the letters. She couldn't tell if Victoria was there. Maybe she'd decided to give them some privacy, Lizzie thought with a smile.

Griff took the tin into his lap and lifted the lid. First, he took out the ring, letting the gold band sit on the tip of his index finger, his man's hand making it seem small. Then he tucked it safely back into the felt, and tucked the felt into the tin. Lizzie loved him for the respect he showed each object, the delicacy with which he took a letter from the centre of the pile and began to read.

'My darling, you make a very nice sausage roll . . . '

He paused, quirking an eyebrow. Lizzie slapped his arm and he grinned and read on:

'Who would have guessed, when I know how resistant you are to the kitchen? Or perhaps it was the starlight last night and the fresh sea air that made everything taste so good. Or perhaps it was the company. I have never been to a midnight picnic that lasted until dawn before. And I have never wanted to leave a place less.

'When I got back to my room, I found your handkerchief in my pocket. I made a wish on it and put it under my pillow like a child with his first infatuation.'

Griff smiled at Lizzie. 'That's cute. I always imagined Victorian men were repressed.'

'I'm starting to like him, too.'

She enjoyed watching Griff as he read. His voice was steady and low and she could stare unashamedly at his lips.

'My time here has come as a revelation to me, and I realise that I didn't know myself at all. I thought I didn't want any kind of entanglements, that it would only add complications to my life. But my love for you is so simple and true it makes everything else clearer, and now I can't bear to think of being without it.'

Griff lowered the paper. His eyes were serious and soft.

'This redeems him somewhat, eh?' he said.

'Well, I'd marry him,' Lizzie said.

Griff laughed. 'Oh, would you? Be careful, someone listening might get jealous!'

Lizzie clasped her hands over her mouth. Then she said, 'It's ok, I don't think she's here.'

'I wasn't talking about Victoria,' Griff whispered, leaning towards her.

She bowed her head shyly as he slid nearer to her, until his chest was against her arm, and she could feel its rise and fall, and his breath tickling her ear. She pressed into the warmth of him, but still she paused, knowing she only had to lift her head to take what he was offering. He waited, patient as the moon.

It was the moment, Lizzie knew, to plunge into her future. It was a silver six-pence moment.

She let the sweet-sharp longing that had been a part of her since the first time she saw him string out until it was unbearable. And then she lifted her face to his, and felt his lips on hers.

23

Time eventually moved onwards. Lizzie remembered what had brought her up to the roof in the first place.

'I can't risk having Victoria ruin our opening night,' she told Griff. 'I have to find some way to communicate with her, to find out what she wants. I can't get any further with just letters and scrapbooks.'

Griff immediately looked unhappy. They were sitting cross-legged opposite one another on the roof, and he had his hands on her knees in a way that was familiar and easy, and very distracting to Lizzie.

'The only times you could see her before were when . . . ' He trailed off.

'I know. It's not exactly pleasant. But I'm talking about perhaps pricking my finger or something, not leaping off the roof.'

'Is there really no other way?'

'Can you think of any?'

He sighed and didn't answer.

'Will you stay with me while I do it?' she asked. 'Of course. I'm not going to let you do it alone.' She smiled, relieved. She didn't want him to

know how nervous she was. She wasn't even sure how she was going to find the courage to cut herself, no matter how small the wound.

'I could do it,' Griff said suddenly. 'My blood made you feel faint too, didn't it? I'll cut myself, then you won't have to.'

'No, Griff, I'm not going to let you do that — '

'You'll have enough to worry about, if your blood pressure drops . . .' He frowned again. 'Are we really sure there's no other way?'

They fell quiet, thinking. Neither of them was keen on the idea, but Lizzie didn't know of any other option.

Unless . . .

She sat up straighter, an idea forming.

'Remember when you told me — '

Griff's phone let out a peal of notes from his pocket and he took it out to read the screen.

'Sorry, it's Waverley.'

He answered the call, and Lizzie listened while he explained to Waverley where he was. Then she saw his face fall, and he said, 'No, he's not with me. Do you mean you haven't seen him?'

He stood up, turned in am anxious circle, pushing his hand into his hair and tugging at his scalp. 'No, of course — he'll be upset after Mia . . . but he was supposed to come straight back into the house to you.'

Lizzie stood up too, put a light, reassuring hand on Griff's arm.

'I'll be right down,' Griff said, before hanging up.

'Oscar?' Lizzie said.

'I should have been there . . . '

He crossed the roof, half skidded down the bank to the ground. Lizzie hurried to catch up to him; he reached out a hand to help her the last few feet.

'He's probably found some quiet hiding place for a bit of time alone,' Lizzie said.

'Yes, probably.' But he didn't seem convinced.

'What is it?' she asked, noticing his hesitation.

'The way I left things with Mia . . . If she wanted to get back at me . . . '

'You think she might have taken him after all?'

Griff's skin had a sickly tinge, as if the possibility made him nauseous. 'I'm going to go back and check if any of his things are gone.'

Lizzie squeezed his arm. 'Go. I'll catch up with you.'

He nodded distractedly, but before she let go of him, she said, 'Try not to worry. We'll find him. I'm sure of it.'

He gave her a grateful look, and started towards the house. Lizzie hung back, thinking.

She was more perturbed than she let Griff know. The niggling feeling of disquiet that she had carried with her for days was stronger than ever. She'd put it down to Victoria's disruption and unpredictability, but the truth was she had a sense of dread, that something bad was pending and she couldn't see what it was, and wouldn't have any hope of stopping it until she figured out what she was missing. Something was wrong. And it wasn't entirely to do with Victoria.

For a start, Oscar had promised her that he wouldn't leave without speaking to Griff first, and she trusted him to keep his word. And though she understood Griff's fears, she didn't believe Mia would use Oscar that way either. Mia knew Oscar was happy here.

So he must be holed up in some secret place, gathering his thoughts, she told herself, thinking of the time the two of them had hidden from the world together in the summerhouse.

She really hoped that was what it was.

She returned to the half-formed plan she'd been about to discuss with Griff, feeling it out while she followed the direction Griff had taken to the house. But instead of going to the entrance, she went around the side of the building, to visit the pear tree.

Remember when you told me Mia had eaten a pear from the tree once? she had been about to say to Griff. And it put her to sleep . . .

The pear tree was full of fruit, as if it was expecting her. She stood under its heavy boughs and, reaching up, plucked a pear from its clasp with a gentle tug. Its grainy skin was golden yellow with a faint blush of sun-kissed pink. It was warm in her hand and smelled sweet and fresh. But maybe that was just her memory and imagination, filling in the knowledge of what a pear should be.

She sat at the base of the tree, the fruit in her palm, her scattered pulse telling her of the danger of it.

'Remember,' she whispered to the tree, 'you're friendly.'

She took a big bite of the pear.

★ ★ ★

Lizzie wasn't aware of passing out, or falling asleep, or any transition at all, she only knew she was dreaming. But not dreaming.

The sky was dark, the moon a hazy light behind cloud. She heard hushed giggling, and when she looked up through the branches of the tree over her head, she saw a pair of male legs stepping across a thick bough, and a woman's arms reaching for him from the window above, drawing him in. He made a clumsy movement, and there was a breathless shriek from her, and a quick 'Shh!' from him, and them more whispers and giddy laughter before his shadowed figure disappeared into the open window.

Alone now, Lizzie pushed herself up from the base of the tree. The sky immediately began to lighten. By the time she had walked across the garden, it felt like midday, though she couldn't feel the sun on her, or the summer air.

She followed the sound of voices and laughter and came upon a group of people outside the summerhouse. Two young women and two young men were preforming in front of an audience of a dozen or so others, who were seated around a tea table. Everyone was quite merry, except for one heavy-set older man in the audience, who looked on with a scowl.

Victoria was one of the women on stage. She wore her white summer gown. Her face was glowing as she offered her hand to a smart young man, who bowed to kiss it, and then pulled her to him with an arm around her waist.

Even if Lizzie hadn't known anything about these two people, the way that their touch lingered and their eyes met with mischief and secret communications would have given away that they weren't acting.

She wasn't the only one to notice.

'I think that will do,' the older man in the audience cut in aggressively, getting to his feet.

The cheerful atmosphere was broken; the performers broke apart and stood dumbly as those in the audience shifted uncomfortably, wondering how to continue. The older man with all the authority stalked back to the house.

Victoria's cheeks were burning, but Lizzie couldn't tell if it was from humiliation or fury.

Just as if she were in a dream, those final words echoed after the man who had spoken them was gone:

That will do . . . That will do . . .

The end of everything, Lizzie thought.

She turned to see where the man had gone, and saw instead Victoria's figure walking ahead of her, towards the house. She had a shawl on now, of yellow wool, and her hair was loose on her shoulders.

Victoria glanced back over her shoulder and looked directly at Lizzie. Taking the cue, Lizzie followed after her.

The main door to the house was ajar. Victoria had disappeared inside by the time Lizzie reached it, and she could hear distinct voices inside:

'I will not have that behaviour from my daughter! And I will not have a man in my house who would take advantage of my hospitality!'

Lizzie heard feminine voices: Victoria's steady tone, and another woman —Victoria's mother perhaps — although Lizzie couldn't make out their words.

'I know exactly what he is,' the man continued. 'He has had the audacity to question me on numerous occasions. And you are to inform him he has outstayed his welcome, Victoria, or I shall. I want him out of the house before tomorrow night. I have more important things to think about!'

Lizzie pushed the door open, almost surprised when she was able to shift the heavy oak, but when she could see inside the house, it was empty. Eerily so. Not as if people had just left it, but as though no one had been inside for centuries.

She couldn't bring herself to go in. Instead, she turned back from the door.

Victoria, in her yellow shawl, was now on the lawn, this time heading in the direction of the cove.

Lizzie chased after her, but Victoria was always too far ahead to catch. When Lizzie got to the edge of the garden, Victoria was disappearing down the footpath.

'Wait!' Lizzie called. 'What are you trying to tell me?'

At the beach, it was twilight. She knew there was a strong breeze because the grasses were bending under it and the waves sounded of conflict and drama, but again she didn't feel any of it on her skin. As she rounded the cliff path, the beach opened up to her, and she saw Victoria and Thomas on the shore below.

He had hold of her hand; their heads were bent close to each other as he put the emerald ring on to her finger. She pulled him to her and rested her head on his chest, her hands fisted in the fabric of his shirt as if she would never let him go.

Lizzie thought they were alone, but a scraping and banging from further along the beach drew her notice. It wasn't the natural sound of something being washed up by the waves. Cautiously, she left the path and stepped onto the sand, and found she was moving into night-time again, under a cloud-thick sky.

She turned back to Victoria and Thomas, but they were gone. The suspicious noises continued. Lizzie wanted to know what was causing them, but dread in the pit of her stomach made it hard to move.

Lieutenant Thomas Madden was braver than she was. He was full dressed in his uniform now, handsome and young and fearless, and he moved right past Lizzie from the footpath, so near he might have brushed her arm. For a moment he paused, listening, frowning as he identified the sound. And then he continued on, purposefully marching towards the smugglers' tunnel.

Lizzie was frozen to the spot with apprehension. She wanted to call out to him not to go.

There's always been something about that tunnel . . .

Her whole body was cold now, as if she really were standing on the beach at midnight. The sound came again: the thump of a wooden barrel being unloaded from a boat; the scrape of it being rolled around the rocks. And this time, a shout.

Lizzie started running towards the tunnel. Her feet hit the sand soundlessly and left no imprint behind.

At the mouth of the cave, three or four men had been working to unload a small boat moored there. Two of them were now heading into the tunnel, not with their contraband cargo, but with Thomas slumped between them, one of their arms hooked under each of his. Dragging his unconscious body into the cave.

Lizzie forced herself to continue forwards, but she couldn't make herself go inside after them. She heard a sickening thud that turned her stomach. She had to stop to lean a hand on the rock. It was too late for Thomas. This was why Victoria never saw him again. Everyone had thought so badly of him, when all along he'd been trying to do something heroic: trying to catch the smugglers.

A low rumble of laughter came from inside the tunnel. It wasn't the same laughter that Lizzie had heard before, but it reminded her of it — it had the same note of cruelty. She backed away in disgust. At the mouth of the cave the litter with the cigarette packet she'd noticed before shook itself in the wind, trying to break free of the reeds.

The cigarette packet.

All the pieces came together, and a sudden kick of revelation sent Lizzie reeling with a gasp. Like a fish caught on a line, she snapped backwards until it felt somehow she collided with her own self she'd left sitting under the pear tree, and she opened her eyes to the mid-afternoon of the present day, understanding everything.

24

The last place she wanted to go was back to the smugglers' tunnel. But she had to. She ran across the gardens, back to the path to the cove, puzzling things out as she went and hoping she was wrong. She thought again of Oscar promising not to leave without a word. She remembered all the occasions at Hartley when she'd felt like she was being watched, and had assumed it was Victoria. She thought of Mia denying having stolen Meredith's cigarette case, or having left the flat, even.

And finally, she remembered the litter at the tunnel, and the campfire that had been set inside, and the laughter that she'd heard when she'd already been so on edge . . . Just how long had Adam been stalking them all?

* * *

She came to a breathless halt at the end of the footpath. There, hunched against the cliff that housed the tunnel, she saw Oscar. She almost collapsed in relief.

But Oscar, noticing her, made frantic gestures for her to hide and keep quiet.

Lizzie hunkered down in the grasses at the bottom of the path and listened. She could hear a man and a woman arguing. When she peeped out, she saw Adam coming in and out of view as he paced the sand near the mouth of the tunnel.

Now that she knew Oscar was all right, Lizzie wasn't quite so scared. She could tell that he was, though. So she waited until a moment when Adam was out of sight and distracted by his argument, and then she dashed over to Oscar.

Oscar put his finger to his lips desperately. She nodded to reassure him, and he flung himself into her arms, trembling like a frightened kitten. What did he know about Adam that Lizzie didn't?

Lizzie took his tear-stained face in her hands and whispered, 'It's ok. It's ok now. Go back to the house, Griff's looking for you — '

He shook his head. 'I'm not leaving Mum.' His small fingers dug into her arm. 'He wants the ring, and she hasn't got it.'

Lizzie pulled him a step further away from the tunnel, putting herself in his place. 'Someone has to get help, and you're a much faster runner than I am. I'll stay. Ok?'

He hesitated, but eventually nodded. Lizzie peeped around the rock. She could still hear Adam's voice, but he wasn't in sight. She gave Oscar a gentle push and he took off across the beach, racing back to the house.

She allowed herself a second to imagine how pleased Griff would be to see him. Reflexively, she reached into her pocket for her phone. It wasn't there; it was in her bag, which was still on the roof of the summerhouse.

'I don't believe you would be so careless with something that valuable,' she heard Adam say in a cold voice. 'It's not like you, Mia.'

Lizzie took a risk and peered again around the rock. Adam was a little way from the mouth of the cave, with his back to Lizzie. Mia's rucksack was open on the ground in front of him, its contents strewn across the sand. He kicked aside a pair of shoes and turned over a crumpled t-shirt with the toe of his dirty boot.

'What is it you're not telling me?' he demanded.

Mia was in front of the cave, standing with her arms wrapped around herself. The corner of her mouth was swollen and her lip was split. As if she'd been struck.

She glanced up and saw Lizzie. Their eyes connected. Mia looked quickly away, her expression blank.

'There's nothing I'm not telling you,' she told Adam.

Lizzie flattened herself against the rock again before Adam turned around.

'I want that ring!' he roared, the deep boom of his voice making every muscle in Lizzie's body tense as if she were under attack.

He made a move towards Mia. Lizzie stepped out from behind the cliff to show herself, and Adam drew up short.

'It's not yours, though, is it?' Lizzie said in an even voice.

She was terrified and couldn't pretend otherwise, but right then she was angry enough at him too, for scaring Oscar and bullying Mia, that it was keeping her fear in check.

Adam appraised her with interest. His beard had grown since she last saw him, and his expression was so unfeeling that she wondered how he had ever seemed good looking. 'What would you know about it?'

Lizzie didn't answer. Adam glanced past her, to check she was alone.

'Mia owes me that ring,' he said. 'It's between us.'

'Except it's not Mia's ring, either.'

He gave a wry smile, the kind that warned his patience was wearing thin.

'I'm going to ask you again: what would you know about it?'

He slowly advanced towards her. His

scent carried the same tang as the washed up bladderwrack on the tide line. Lizzie edged towards Mia, aware Adam was putting himself in a position to block her escape back to the beach.

'Oh, I get it,' he said. 'You know where it is, don't you? Have you got my ring, gorgeous?'

'You should leave,' Lizzie said. 'People know that you're here now . . .'

He laughed. There it was: the same laughter she'd heard coming from the tunnel that day.

'Is that so?' he said. 'Maybe you and I should go somewhere else, then?' He lurched forward and grabbed Lizzie's wrist. She tried to pull free, but he squeezed more tightly, until she felt he would quite happily snap the bone if she pushed him to it. She could sense the will in him to do it; his complete indifference to her as a human being in her own right. So she stopped resisting.

Mia leapt forward and tried to force Adam away from Lizzie. He shoved her with his free hand. She fell backwards onto the sand, landing heavily.

'No, here's what you're going to do,' he told Mia. 'You're going to use all those sneaky skills of yours to get back into that house, and you're going to bring me everything of value that you can carry. Everything. Because if you don't, I'm going to come back here one night and I'm going to burn the whole place to the ground, and I don't care who's inside when I do it.'

Mia's face turned white. She glared up at him in hatred.

He turned his attention back to Lizzie, wrenching her arm until she winced.

'You, I'm keeping hold of. We're going to have a little chat.'

Mia slowly got to her feet.

'Keep your mouth shut while you're gone,' he ordered Mia.

Mia looked wearily at Lizzie, as if in apology. Lizzie didn't blame her if she wanted to save herself. In Mia's position, Lizzie would be tempted to do the same. She would rather Mia run away from here and keep running, rather than steal from Hartley to satisfy Adam.

But she really didn't want to be alone with him.

Mia, thankfully, had a different idea. Her fist flew out from behind her back, opening up to throw an explosion of gritty sand into Adam's face.

Spluttering, Adam let go of Lizzie. Mia grabbed her just as fast, pulling her after her into the mouth of the tunnel.

'Keep hold of me,' Mia said, transferring Lizzie's grasp to the back of her shirt. Lizzie held tight. 'I've been along here dozens of times. Have you got a light?'

'I left my phone at the house,' Lizzie said breathlessly. 'You?'

'Adam took it.'

They turned a corner and in moments were in total darkness. Lizzie caught her toe on the uneven ground and pitched forward, stumbling into Mia, turning them both around.

'It's ok,' Mia said, righting her. 'I think it's this way.'

Lizzie could feel Mia groping with

her arms outstretched. The swish of her fingers trailing the walls. She could hear her own breath, fast and jagged.

Suddenly Mia drew up short.

'What is it?' Lizzie whispered.

'It's a dead end. I took a wrong turn . . . This must be one of the places they dug out the hide the contraband . . .'

Lizzie reached out a tentative hand. She felt the slightly slimy rock face, and then, lower, something that felt more like packed earth, and even the soft rotten corner of a wooden strut. Taking a step, she stubbed her toe again. It was hard even to picture the shape of the space they were in, let alone how to get out.

Worse, they heard Adam shouting, and saw the travelling glow of his torch beam at the far end of the tunnel as it cut into the blackness.

'We have to move before he finds us,' Mia whispered, panic in her voice.

Lizzie reached out for her. Her touch found Mia's arm, and she followed it to Mia's hand, grasping her tightly.

'Victoria?' she whispered. 'Are you

there? Can you help us find the way out?'

The bobbing torchlight was dancing closer. It gave Lizzie only the merest sense of the landscape around them; by the time it gave them enough light to move by, Adam would be too close to outrun.

'Is anyone here?' Lizzie said desperately. She took a wild chance: 'Thomas . . .'

Something ephemeral brushed against her left hand. She almost yelped.

'What's wrong?' Mia said.

Lizzie took a breath. 'Thomas?' she said. 'Lieutenant Thomas Madden . . . I know you're there . . .'

It was such a cold touch. But it was a gentle hand that closed over hers. She let it draw her forward, and brought Mia after her.

The hand gave a tug on hers, but it almost moved through her, as if it was dissolving.

'I know you're there,' she said again, remembering how Victoria had become stronger each time Lizzie acknowledged her. 'Thomas.'

The hand took a firmer grip, guiding them through the passageway. Lizzie held her breath and trusted.

Eventually they saw daylight ahead. The opening of the tunnel behind the folly. At the same moment, the beam from Adam's torch swept over them.

For the briefest moment, Lizzie saw the figure of a man beside them: young, uniformed, heroic. He looked at her with yearning. But it was just a flash before the light was gone, and Mia pushed at her frantically. 'Go! Go!'

They broke into a run towards the patch of daylight. In seconds, they were out and clambering through the overgrowth at the mouth of the tunnel, and then speeding up the steps of the folly.

Mia was ahead of Lizzie now, but she reached back for her, grabbing her hand again. They raced across the grass together.

The mid-afternoon light was doing strange things; at first Lizzie thought it was a trick of her vision caused by coming out of the darkness into the sun. As they got nearer to the house, she understood what it was: the strobing blue lights of two police cars parked on the driveway.

25

They caught Adam trying to escape on the smugglers' route into town. The police arrested him for assault and theft, and added a charge for skipping probation. It was enough to keep Mia safe from him for a long while.

By that time Griff had raced back from the cove, where he must have arrived just after they all disappeared into the tunnel. He barrelled straight towards Lizzie and Mia with all his reserve stripped from him.

It was Lizzie he went to first, scooping her up, lifting her feet clear off the ground. She'd never been hugged so tight in her life.

She'd have been happy if he never let go.

Meanwhile, Mia was kneeling in the grass giving the same treatment to Oscar, who had been waiting with Waverley as the police arrived and was only a step behind Griff.

'Are you all right?' Mia asked him. 'My little hero.' Griff drew back to take Lizzie's face in his hands. 'Are you all right? Were you hurt?'

'I'm fine. Mia saved me.'

Griff turned to Mia. She gave a modest shrug. He went to her, touched a gentle finger to her bruised jaw. Then he pulled her to him while she was still crouched and kissed the top of her head. She let him do it. For a minute the three of them — Griff, Mia, and Oscar — were intertwined. Still family.

It wasn't something Lizzie had to compete with. It was beautiful. 'My goodness, Lizzie!'

Meredith approached from the driveway, with Kate and Fatima behind her. 'What on earth is going on?'

Lizzie looked at her sister sheepishly. They were supposed to be having a meeting with the theatre group. She'd messed up their plans, again.

★ ★ ★

They all went to the restaurant, where Claudette provided nourishing food, police officers took statements, and Mia and Lizzie related everything that had happened. When she got to the point in the story where Thomas guided them out of the tunnel, Mia simply said, 'Somehow we made it through in the dark. I guess I just remembered the way.'

Lizzie smiled into her cup of coffee. Mia knew every part of Hartley, almost better than anyone else. She'd climbed the pear tree; she'd eaten its fruit. She knew exactly what had happened in the tunnel.

As everyone chatted and unwound from the drama of the day, Lizzie sat back and gazed around the restaurant. Her friends were taking up two tables between them. Beyond that, other customers were enjoying meals with family and friends, taking a break from the drama in their own lives. Lizzie felt safe and contented, and she was proud of Griff for creating a place so welcoming.

She caught Waverley's eye. He was at

the end of the table with his arm around Oscar's shoulders, as if he intended never to let him out of his sight again. He gave her a curious nod, and she smiled. He obviously knew there was something missing from Mia's story too.

In the next day or two she'd have to find a moment to fill Waverley in on his true family history.

It was late in the evening by the time they left the restaurant. Lizzie walked out into the fresh air with Meredith. The sky was pink and orange at the horizon.

'We didn't get any work done today,' Lizzie noted hesitantly.

'That's ok,' Meredith said, putting her jacket on and scooping her hair out from under her collar in a smooth gesture. 'We'll talk about things in the morning. I'm pretty sure we're going to be fantastic tomorrow anyway.'

Lizzie lit up happily. 'Good. Me too.'

'It's not life and death, right?' She cocked her head, then stepped forward to hug Lizzie. 'Did I ever tell you I'm proud of you?'

'No, never.'

'Maybe one day I will.' She let Lizzie go. 'Ready to go home?'

'There's something I have to do first. You go, I'll catch up.'

'You're sure? I'd wait, but I'm meeting Jerome . . .'

Lizzie raised a questioning eyebrow. Meredith shrugged nonchalantly. 'We had an actual chat. Bit of a miscommunication before; turns out he actually loves travelling. He says if I have to go anywhere for work, he doesn't mind how far he has to travel to see me.'

'Sounds promising.'

'Yes,' Meredith said bashfully. 'It does. He's quite something when I can get him to actually open his mouth.' She did a slow, whimsical turn on the driveway. 'Go and do what you have to do. I'll be waiting at home when you get there.'

'Thanks Meredith.'

'Always.'

★ ★ ★

It was harder to climb the bank behind the summerhouse in the dark, especially when Lizzie was fatigued and aching from the events of the day. Her wrist, where Adam had caught hold of her, was so bruised she couldn't lean on it as she climbed, but cradled it against her chest.

Remembering the cold indifference with which Adam caused harm made Lizzie's heart jitter with fear all over again. She appreciated Mia's bravery in standing up to him all the more.

Once she got to the summerhouse roof there was more light to see by. She collected her things, picking up her bag and checking her phone. Then she made sure the ring and the letters were tightly sealed in the tin, before setting about putting it back into its hiding place.

Fifteen years it had been missing from this spot: the period that Waverley said the estate went through its 'bad patch', Lizzie mused. Maybe the turnaround of its fortunes had something to do with Oscar returning it to the grounds at Hartley months ago . . .

Or maybe that was just her imagination running away with her again.

If Victoria was watching her as she buried the tin, Lizzie couldn't tell. She wondered if she would ever see her again. Just in case she wasn't alone, she whispered, 'I know the truth now.' But there was no answer in the silence around her.

She was replacing the stonework in front of the tin when she heard someone else climbing up the bank. Griff, she thought, with immediate joy. But she was surprised, when the person emerged, to see that it was Mia.

Mia stopped at the edge of the roof and nodded to the hiding place.

'Is the ring back there?'

Lizzie almost hesitated, but she felt Mia deserved better than her distrust now. 'It is,' she said.

'Good.'

Mia came closer, perched on the head of a decorative column.

'I always felt guilty about taking it. That's why I never sold it. But I liked looking at it sometimes. It was a little bit of security, I suppose. Like a promise.'

It was a promise to someone else, Lizzie thought. But knowing something about the instability of Mia's world, she could understand what Mia meant.

'I'll tell Waverley that it's here,' Lizzie said. 'He ought to know. But I think he'll probably let it stay where it is.'

Mia nodded, as if she saw nothing strange in that, either.

'What did Adam mean when he said that you owed it to him?' Lizzie asked.

'It was supposed to be compensation. I was the one who told the police about his criminal enterprise and got him sent to prison.' She glanced at Lizzie. 'I had to get him away from Oscar somehow.'

Lizzie couldn't imagine how hard that decision had been. Nearly as hard as asking Griff to take Oscar, probably.

'He seemed so nice when I first met him,' Mia murmured, almost to herself.

Lizzie moved to sit beside her and the two of them watched the sun set over the estate. Lizzie wondered about the other tenants of the house, the people going about their daily lives. She and Mia were never more than visitors here, but surely they knew the house more deeply than most.

'Oscar's a real success story,' she said softly.

They didn't look at one another, but she felt Mia's smile.

'Isn't he, though?' Mia said.

$$\star \quad \star \quad \star$$

'Hey, you two!'

Lizzie gazed down to see Griff standing on the path below them.

'What's so interesting up there?' he called.

Lizzie and Mia shared a glance.

'Just coming!' Lizzie called back.

She started to make her way down to him, but Mia didn't follow. She gestured for Lizzie to go ahead.

'He's all yours,' she said.

Lizzie recognised the generosity of the act. She paused at the edge of the roof.

'I hope you'll stay for a couple more

days,' she said. 'Come and see the play with Oscar tomorrow night.'

Mia shrugged. 'I'll see what I can do.' But Lizzie sensed she was pleased to be asked.

'Maybe the house will be nicer to me now,' Mia mused.

When Lizzie reached Griff, he took her hand and pulled her around the corner, out of Mia's sight. It was the first time they'd been alone all evening.

He lifted her damaged wrist gently in his palm and bowed his head to kiss the purpling bruise, so delicately that she felt it in her heart more
than on her skin.

'Are you really all right?' he whispered.

'I am. Everything's ok.'

'And Victoria . . . ?'

'She's quiet. I think she may have been trying to warn me about Adam as much as to tell me about Thomas.'

He pressed his lips to her forehead and she felt all his tender concern for her; all the worry he'd been through earlier.

'I can't stay,' he said, though he looked

at her with longing. 'I've got to get back to Oscar.'

'Just a moment, then,' she said, pulling his head down to hers. She felt his smile against her lips.

'Just a moment . . .'

26

It was nearly time for Curtain Up. The garden was full of families and couples and groups of friends picnicking and pouring drinks and taking photos of the house as its white façade glowed golden in reflection of the lowering sun.

In the summerhouse Kate was doing vocal warm-ups, and Daniel was doing physical ones. It was all getting quite crowded, so Lizzie stepped outside.

She didn't mean to intrude on Meredith and Jerome, who were around the corner, near the fish pond. He'd brought Meredith a bouquet of roses, and she was explaining how she usually got flowers after the show, but she was very grateful, and pink roses were her favourite . . .

'Sorry,' she said, 'I'm babbling. It's because I'm nervous.' Lizzie withdrew before they noticed her, though she couldn't resist a quick glance back. 'I know I'm quiet,' she heard Jerome say softly to Meredith, 'but I like to hear your voice.'

Meredith, on her tiptoes, threw her arms around his neck . . . And then Lizzie really did have to move on and give them privacy.

As nervous as they all were about the opening night, there were plenty of reminders that other things were important in life too, which put their nerves into perspective.

Meredith had had another piece of good news that morning: the police came to the house to ask her to identify her silver cigarette case, which had been with Adam's belongings.

They also took Lizzie aside to tell her what they found in their search of the tunnel.

'We came across human remains buried in one of the dug-out sections,' the detective sergeant told her. 'It seems they're historic, not recent, and not anything to do with the man we arrested yesterday. Did you know what we would find when you mentioned the tunnel to us?'

'I only thought it might have been used to hide stolen goods,' she said, blushing at the lie even as she said it. 'I noticed in the place where we stopped yesterday that the ground was soft and it seemed like it might have been disturbed.' She cleared her throat. 'But I've been doing some research into the local history of the area, and I think I might be able to help you identify the remains . . . '

All she could do for Thomas now was see that he got a proper burial, and a headstone to be remembered by.

Later, when Lizzie saw Sally, her journalist friend, in the audience, she had another idea.

Surely the uncovering of a skeleton in a smugglers' tunnel was worth a story in the paper? And perhaps Lizzie would be able to use her research to convince Sally that Thomas was actually a hero who died trying to stop crooks and thieves. At least then the truth would be out in the world, even if it was late in coming.

She thought about Victoria, sitting down to write a letter to her lover, not knowing that he was already gone. He might have been on his way to her when he was side-tracked; he may have been about to deliver a note that would explain how they could be together. Victoria had never known, not for as long as she lived.

And then, in death, how long had she stood at the entrance to the tunnel, pining?

Maybe time moved differently in the afterlife. Lizzie hoped so.

She was about to go back into the summerhouse when she saw Oscar running towards her.

'Hi! Did you and your mum get good seats?'

'Yes — right at the front. With Laurel, too.'

She was glad to see him smiling. She'd been worried about him since yesterday. But if anything, he looked more relaxed than he'd seemed in ages.

Sometimes there was a relief in the worst happening — at least you knew it was over.

'This is for you,' he said, handing her

a small jewellery case.

'What is it?'

'Griff asked me to give it to you.' He didn't hang around, whizzing back to his seat, giggling.

Lizzie, pleasantly flushed, looked at the closed box. With everything else going on, she'd barely seen Griff today. She knew he was at the restaurant right now; that some of the customers had chosen to have dinner before seeing the play, and others had booked hampers from Claudette's kitchen to enjoy on the lawn while they watched. Word was getting around about the quality of their food, and Lizzie didn't doubt the restaurant's reputation had cast a good light on her and Meredith's own venture.

Lizzie had been very aware of Griff's nearness all day, despite their separation, and a couple of times she'd walked past the restaurant and had managed to wave to him inside, or had looked up from her work to see him crossing the lawn, as if he'd been hungry for a sight of her just as much as she'd been wanting a glimpse of him.

They had plans to meet up later, but it was touching that he wanted to give her something before the play started, like a good luck token.

Savouring the moment, she opened the box. On the dark velvet inside lay a silver pendant on a chain. The pendant was in the shape of a house, simple and symmetrical, not unlike the basic outline of Hartley House. Lizzie turned it over and found an inscription engraved: *We're all mad here.*

Another quote from Alice's Adventures in Wonderland. She laughed in delight.

I see you, he was telling her with this gift. *Here is a place where you belong.*

★ ★ ★

Meredith returned to the summerhouse, dreamy-eyed and excited, and met Lizzie outside the door.

'Ready?' she asked.

Lizzie glanced through the window

at Daniel, Kate and Fatima, who were giddy and exuberant, all keyed up with energy. The butterflies in her stomach were for each and every one of them.

She nodded at Meredith. 'Ready.'

Earlier that day she'd received an email from Jacintha Buckley, mentioning that she'd like to bring a friend to the performance with her. He knew nothing about the theatre, she said breezily, but was the Chief Executive of a software company and was looking for somewhere to place his corporate sponsorship, and Jacintha had thought of Lizzie and Meredith . . .

It could all come to nothing, of course.

In the end, this run of performances at Hartley House might be all that ever existed of their play.

'If this is it,' Meredith said, her thoughts following the same track as Lizzie's, 'it has still been completely worthwhile. What an experience we've had, eh?'

'What an experience,' Lizzie agreed, touching the pendant where it lay against her collarbone.

Meredith paused with her hand on the

door handle.

'And,' she added, 'there's always that second script of yours on your desk. The one you think I don't know about.'

'Hey!' Lizzie exclaimed, affronted. 'Have you been snooping — ' She stopped. 'Wait . . . Are you saying you want to work with me again?'

Meredith grinned as she let herself into the summerhouse.

'We'll see,' she said. 'Who knows what might happen?'

We do hope that you have enjoyed reading this large print book.

Did you know that all of our titles are available for purchase?

We publish a wide range of high quality large print books including:
Romances, Mysteries, Classics
General Fiction
Non Fiction and Westerns

Special interest titles available in large print are:
The Little Oxford Dictionary
Music Book, Song Book
Hymn Book, Service Book

Also available from us courtesy of Oxford University Press:
Young Readers' Dictionary
(large print edition)
Young Readers' Thesaurus
(large print edition)

For further information or a free brochure, please contact us at:
Ulverscroft Large Print Books Ltd.,
The Green, Bradgate Road, Anstey,
Leicester, LE7 7FU, England.
Tel: (00 44) **0116 236 4325**
Fax: (00 44) **0116 234 0205**

Other titles in the
Linford Romance Library:

LOVE IN LAVENDER LANE

Jill Barry

Fiona exchanges her quiet suburban world for 1970s London when she inherits her great-aunt's marriage bureau near Marble Arch. But she has never been truly in love, so it's going to be a challenge arranging perfect pairings for her starry-eyed clients . . . While Fiona's busy interviewing and arranging introductions, how will she ever find time to make her own dream come true? And could it be that she and her most difficult client to match are actually meant for one another?